ALEX MCKENNA AND THE ACADEMY OF SOULS

ALEX MCKENNA AND THE ACADEMY OF SOULS

VICKI-ANN BUSH

ALSO BY VICKI-ANN BUSH

Alex McKenna and the Geranium Deaths

Alex McKenna & The Academy of Souls – Audiobook

Alex McKenna & A Winter's Night - Audiobook

UNTHREADED

Ophelia

The Garden of Two

Saving A Life

The Queen of IT

Winslow Willow the Woodland Fairy

The Darkest Light

Liminal Space

Short Stories

The Joshua Tree

ALEX MCKENNA

LaBoccetta/Russo Family Tree

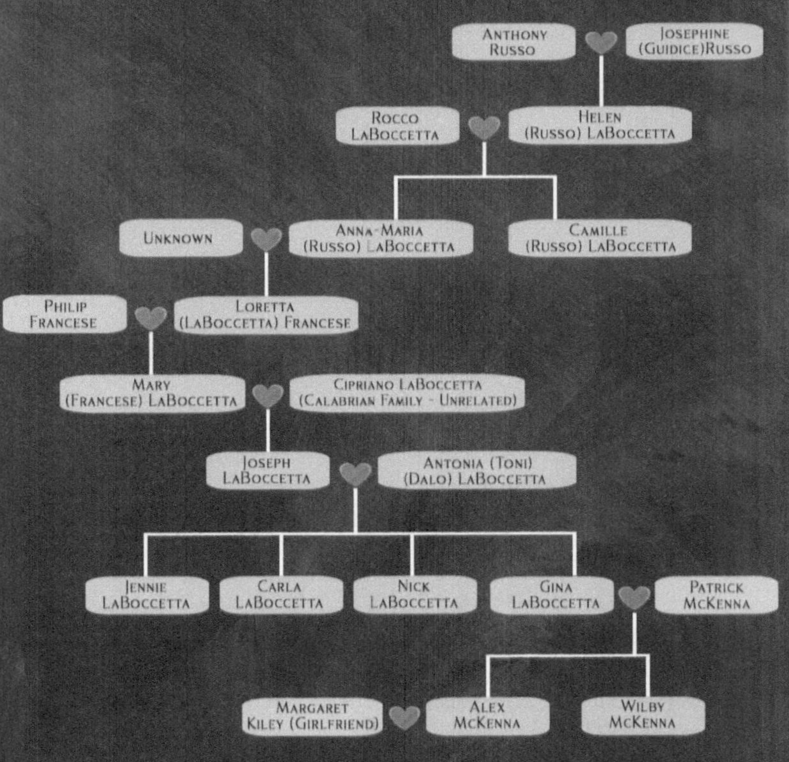

Published in the United States by Creative James Media.

www.creativejamesmedia.com

978-1-956183-27-6 (trade paperback)

First U.S. Edition 2024

This book is dedicated to my cousin, Mary Santucci-SanSeverino. The universe had a plan, and although taking you much too soon hurt those close to you, I have to believe it needed a bright light to navigate the dark days. And you, beautiful girl, were a beacon in the storm. My memories are sprinkled through years of distance, but our childhood is forever preserved in my heart. Thanks for the overalls.

"All that is gold does not glitter,
Not all those who wander are lost;
The old that is strong does not wither,
Deep roots are not reached by the frost."
J.R.R. Tolkien

WELCOME TO THE ACADEMY OF SOULS

Alex scooped his hands underneath Margaret's bottom and pulled her onto his lap.

"Hey McKenna, what do you think you're doing?" she pretended to push him away.

"Just getting warm," Alex flashed her a grin and pulled her closer. "It's extra chilly tonight and I've waited a long time to do this with you."

I know what you mean," Margaret snuggled close. "We were friends and then … I like us this way better."

Margaret curled her arms around his neck and gently kissed it and then his cheek. "Unfortunately, I have to go home."

"Really? I thought we were gonna watch a movie." Alex held her tighter.

"No. *You* thought we were gonna watch a movie. I told you I needed to finish studying for that test tomorrow," she said. "Thank the gods there's only a few weeks left before Christmas vacation. I'm worn out. Speaking of which, you'd better get some sleep tonight. The dark circles under your eyes may be very

Zombie, but they don't look good on you." Margaret placed her hands on his chest and pushed herself up.

"Ouch. A zombie, huh?"

"Well if the drool fits. Come on, walk me to the door please." Margaret slipped on her gray wool coat.

"I'll walk you to the car. Let me grab my hoodie." Alex pulled a black hoodie off the edge of the couch.

"Always the gentlemen." She blew him a kiss.

The open door released a gush of arctic air, plastering an icy veil over their bodies.

"Jesus. Damn it's cold." Alex blew puffs of breath into the night air. Like miniature white clouds, they floated, disappearing under the midnight blue sky.

After Margaret was in the car with the heater blasting, he reached in through the open window and gave her a last kiss goodnight. With promises to text when she got home, he waved as the dark green Honda backed away. Scurrying to get inside, he slammed the door behind him and latched the deadbolt.

No one hated tenth grade as much as Ophelia. Ninth was bad enough, it was the start of four years of horror, but tenth was the middle. Too old to be a kid, too young to be anything else. Of course, that was at the high school she attended before her *beginning*.

At the Academy of Souls, four years could easily turn into an unending loop of history, math, and science. Time could be your worst enemy.

Sitting in the Grand Hall for assembly, Ophelia nervously scanned the aisles for her friends. Unlike them, confidence didn't come easy.

The Grand Hall reminded Ophelia of a short she once saw about Radio City Music Hall in NYC. The red, brocade drapes, and feathery, gold tassels framing the stage and drawing the eye to one of the many rich patterns throughout a masterpiece of design, mimicked the well-known theater. A warm glow, emanating from gas-fueled sconces, reflected the black and gold Victorian wallpaper. Oversized seats, cushioned velvet and stuffed for supreme comfort, filled both levels accommodating the entire student body and staff.

Amry was the first to induct Ophelia into what would become her sanctuary. She was seventeen when she died, only two years older than Ophelia, but they couldn't be more different. Her best friend was fearless, beautiful, and confident. She was the envy of every girl, and the desire for most of the boys. But her striking appearance was only enhanced by her inner beauty. Amry was not a cliché. She was the reason Ophelia was whole. Arriving at the Academy years after the ill-fated day Ophelia and Haven started their beginning, Amry's persistence and kindness lifted her out of the dark lonely place of despair she had chosen to preside in. Amry never gave up on her. Day after day, she'd visit Ophelia in her dorm, and eventually she was able to persuade Headmaster Abernathy to move her into the same room. Amry stayed with her when there were no classes, sometimes in complete silence. Just to be a presence, to show she cared. Eventually Ophelia started to come around. Amry saved her.

Ophelia spotted her gliding down the hall, two aisles over.

"Amry!" Ophelia flailed her arms.

Spinning to find the direction of her friend's voice, Amry grinned when she spotted two pale arms waving above the crowd's heads.

"Hey, where's everybody?" Amry settled in her seat.

"I don't know, but if they are not here soon, the security

crazed Dictator Dick will write them up, and Sam can't afford any more negatives. He doesn't do well confined to the dorms."

Amry slumped down in her seat, twirling the ends of her chestnut hair around her finger. Her translucent green eyes smiled at Ophelia.

"I wonder how he got that name anyway?"

"Richard Cander. Richard—Dick, and he's a power jerk. Dictator Dick, Ophelia grinned.

"You're always so polite, Ophelia." Amry nudged her.

"What do you mean?" Ophelia's eyes widened.

"He's a *power jerk*? Everyone knows he's a mean bastard." "I don't know. Bastard is a strong word. I think he's trying to keep things in order, and sometimes it comes out like he's nasty or doesn't care. But I think it's the opposite. You know I have reservations about using curse words. My mother and father would have been mortified."

"Sometimes I forget you're from 1910. People were so much more relaxed in the 1970's. Before I died in '79, me and my friends were saying some other things far worse than bastard." Amry grinned. "Our little Ophelia, always seeing the good in people. That's what I love about you, Lia," said Amry, using her nickname for Ophelia.

"That's just it, though. If he did, chances are he would have a harder time getting everyone to listen. This way, we may not like him, but he gets the job done." Ophelia frowned.

"Potato, patato. Either way, Sam's ass is grass if he's not here in the next two minutes."

"Whose ass is grass? And why would anyone want an ass made from grass?" Sam plopped in the seat next to Amry

"There you are. Dictator Dick is getting ready to introduce the Headmaster, and you almost missed the opening pledge. You're already skating on thin ice with him. One more, Sam and ..."

"I know. My ass is grass." Sam smirked.

Sam Burkletter was the embodiment of a California boy. Golden blonde locks down to his shoulders, blue green eyes, and a tight surfer's physique. Ophelia bet he was probably tan most of the year when he was living, but now a ghostly white replaced any color life would have given him.

"Hey, what I miss?" Bethany slid next to him.

Bethany Smithson was the doppelganger for the 1970's *it* girl, Farrah Fawcett. Or at least that's what Sam told her. Ophelia didn't know for sure, never seeing Farrah Fawcett, but she took his word for it. It seemed perfect that they had paired up though, two beach beauties from the seventies themselves.

Sam leaned in, softly brushing his lips against Bethany's. A deep blue spark flashed, the result of a small electrical charge when two souls came together.

"Nothing much. We were just discussing the botanical growth on my ass," Sam laughed.

"What?" Bethany's brows furrowed.

"Never mind. He's being an idiot." Amry shook her head. Dictator Dick took center stage, adjusting the microphone to a comfortable level and the lights dimmed twice indicating it was time for silence.

"It is my pleasure to introduce the creator of the Academy of Souls and our beloved Headmaster, Barnabas Abernathy."

Mr. Abernathy appeared on stage in his usual grand entrance. A man with an air for the dramatic stood as smoke billowed around him hazing the purple spotlight circling his frame; all of it a contradiction to his plain black suit. His long white hair pulled back in a neat ponytail, added a softness to the many lines in his face. Abernathy had been around for nearly a thousand years. Joining the old ways of education and blending it with the modern day, he guided with a stern hand but a soft heart.

Standing center stage, he cleared his throat. The raspy

strain resonated into the microphone and drifted out to the enormous room filling the space with command and gaining recognition from the students.

"Attention! Attention everyone! Nice to see you're all looking fine today and on time, Mr. Burkletter." Abernathy eyeballed Sam.

"Right on, Headmaster." Sam flashed a peace sign.

"I wonder why those other men are on stage with him." Ophelia whispered.

"Why and who? They're like the secret service, only not." Amry stretched her neck.

"You having trouble seeing?"

"Yeah. It's okay. I'm not so sure I want to." Amy chuckled.

"What did you mean?" Ophelia leaned in closer.

"Check it out, Lia. Notice they're wearing khakis and golf shirts. Have you ever seen the Secret Service dress like that? I mean on all the occasions they came here attached to some political parody; did they ever wear anything other than a dark suit?"

"You have a point."

"Their clasped hands, straight posture, and scouring of the surroundings, suggests something similar. Maybe military. I guess we're about to find out."

Mr. Abernathy motioned for the two gentlemen to move forward. They stepped up, framing the Headmaster.

"I'd like to introduce Mr. Coal and Mr. Rain." Their benign last names didn't match their ready for action stance. "They'll be monitoring the halls for the next few weeks. Pay no attention to them and continue to go about your daily business. They'll do their best not to interfere with you," he said. "Mr. Coal and Mr. Rain are an addition to the security team. Being entry level sorcerers, I think they'll be a welcome aide to the Academy, and to Mr. Cander, who I'm sure can use the help with some of you unruly students." The Headmaster glared at Roger Mooring, who sat in the first row. A penance he was given because of his outburst at the last assembly.

"Did you see Headmaster look directly at Roger?" Amry whispered, "That boy is nothing but trouble."

"How can you tell it's him? All I see is the back of their heads." Ophelia frowned.

"Because he's the only airhead who would be in the front row and catch the Headmaster's attention. The rest of them are copasetic."

"Now, this brings me to the nature of our assembly today. I need all of you to listen intently to what I'm about to tell you. We'll be getting a new student tomorrow, Zachary Kowal. This is the main reason Mr. Rain and Mr. Coal will be joining us." The Headmaster let his gaze travel from the two men to the teens.

"Mr. Kowal has a dark history. The council wanted to send him directly to *The Nowhere*. But I have hope for him. I'm instructing all of you to stay away from him for now. If he's in your class, be mindful of his presence, but try to avoid engaging. Your safety is very important to me as well. I'll need time to fully assess his capability for rehabilitation. After which, his fate will be determined."

"All right, he's starting to scare me." Ophelia rubbed her forearms.

"Chill. It'll be okay."

Ophelia glanced at her friend. Amry was always the textbook definition of calm. The girl took things as they came. Her motto was, don't sweat the small stuff. They were already dead, how much worse could it really get?

Ophelia wanted to be more like that, but she was born with a very different kind of psyche. In the dictionary, her picture would be right next to the word anxiety.

There was a low buzz of voices echoing through the room. "Quiet, please. When I ask you for complete cooperation, I expect it," demanded the Headmaster.

"That's all for now, you may all go back to class. Except for you, Miss Wetherton, Miss Goodman, Miss Smithson and of course, the fourth member of your merry men, Mr. Burkletter. I would like all of you to meet me in my office promptly." Mr. Abernathy glided off stage.

Ophelia sat unable to speak. She wiped her palms on the sides of her pants. Struggling to swallow past the lump in her throat, she began taking quick shallow breaths.

"Lia, you okay?" Amry rubbed her back.

Ophelia closed her eyes and concentrated on slowing her breathing to a normal pace.

"Damn. I still can't figure out how you do that." Sam stood.

"Sam. Stop it, don't be such a drag." Bethany grabbed his hand and tugged him forward.

"I'm just saying. How is that even possible?"

"Never mind. Come on, let's go." She led him toward the doors.

"You guys go on ahead. We'll be there in a minute." Amry smiled.

Ophelia knew why Sam was confused. She was confused. It never made any sense how anxiety could still overwhelm her. And the breathing, she couldn't even begin to understand where that came from.

"Hey, it's okay. We'll stay here as long as we need to." Amry caressed Ophelia's hair.

"We better go. I don't want Abernathy to be upset with us." Ophelia got up.

Floating up the aisle, the only thought Ophelia could focus on was, *why did the Headmaster pick them? And what for?*

The halls were brimming with chatter from students rushing to class, but all Ophelia could see were the large double Mahogany doors leading into Abernathy's office.

The Headmaster's office was a close second to the Grand Hall when it came to luxury. A century-old cherry desk was the focal point of the room. Headmaster Abernathy was seated, hands folded, and posture erect. Mr. Coal and Mr. Rain were on the left side of the room, each man sat on a yellow and blue, oral wing-back chair. They were as stiff in the office as they had been on stage. Dictator Dick was a different story. His grin was so wide, the Cheshire cat would've been jealous. He took up space in a small chair to the right.

"Come in children. Sit, please." Headmaster motioned toward a plush four-cushion couch with a light blue paisley print, positioned in front of his desk.

Ophelia trembled. She hated confrontation of any kind. She wedged herself between Amry and Bethany. The friend sandwich was comforting.

"I'm sure you're wondering why I called you here. I need more eyes and ears than we have available right now. I'm not asking you to befriend Mr. Kowal, just keep a watchful eye."

"Why us?" Sam leaned forward.

"None of you display any initiative to be a part of other social activities. Other than the time you spend together, you keep to you yourselves. You won't attract unwanted attention."

"So, what, we're on the chopping block now?" Sam's tone was snarky, "You said this guy is dangerous."

"That is precisely why I'm asking you to merely observe. You can report to me anything out of the ordinary that you might witness this boy do. However, you must keep this little assignment quiet. Understood?"

Sam reluctantly nodded.

Ophelia looked over at Amry who was frowning. "Mr.

Abernathy?" Ophelia timidly raised her hand. "Ophelia my dear, this isn't a classroom. Put your hand down and speak."

"What has this boy done?"

"Done?" Mr. Abernathy raised a brow.

"You said he was bad in life, and you trying to save him," Ophelia squeaked.

"I believe his life on earth wasn't a good one. He was thrown into the world with no one. His mother died when he was barely six years old; being forced to fend for himself from such an early age hardened him. I want to try and give him the chance in death he didn't have in life. I am trying to redeem his soul." Abernathy crossed his hands on the desk.

Ophelia looked away. The thought of a soul being sent to *The Nowhere,* churned the faux acids in her stomach. "Headmaster, isn't our safety important? I don't understand?"

"I don't think any of us do, Lia." Amry stood. "What's really going on?"

"Tone, Miss Goodman." Mr. Abernathy hu ed, "This is a delicate matter that will need your..."

"Stop. Just tell us." Amry folded her arms.

"This is bogus, quit taking the long way around," Sam said firmly.

"Zachary Kowal is my sister's son. I promised her right before she crossed over that I would do everything to save him."

The four gasped. Ophelia locked eyes with Amry as she slid back into her space on the couch, and the room fell silent.

Headmaster Abernathy nodded at Dictator Dick. He turned to an oversized étagère on the wall behind his chair and opened the perfectly crafted doors to reveal six drawers. Sliding open the first storage box, he pulled out a manila folder and placed it on the desk in front of the teens.

"Open it." Mr. Abernathy nodded his head.

Amry reached out and flipped the folder revealing multiple sheets of paper.

"All your questions can be answered in this letter. We will give you a few minutes to review it, and then the rest is up to you."

After the four men left the room, the group huddled together reading the contents of the damned boy's life.

"This guy's past reads like a gangster rap sheet. Robbery, assault—*kidnapping*! We're all gonna wind up in *The Nowhere* because he's gonna put us there," Sam exclaimed.

"Sam's right. We're screwed." Bethany slouched down in the seat.

"Zachary Kowal is the son of Marianne Abernathy. Huh ..." Ophelia bit her lip.

"What's huh?" Sam leaned in.

"He died a long time ago; I wonder why Headmaster didn't bring him here sooner?"

"Who cares?" Sam furrowed his brow.

"It's just weird, that's all." Ophelia kept reading. "Says Zachary was banished to the in-between for over five hundred years. I wonder what that is?" Ophelia's eyes widened.

"Sort of like a doorway. On one side your room, on the other, the dorm hallway. He was standing directly in the doorway." Amry grinned. "There are many in-betweens. It just depends on which one he was sent to. I mean what he saw on either side. Either way it's a cruddy existence. You're basically trapped in a world of nothing."

"How did you know that?" Ophelia asked.

"Right after I got here, I met a student who was rescued from one of the in-between worlds. He accidentally slipped into a portal that had been opened by Headmaster. Don't ask me why he opened it, I don't know," she paused and after a moment she continued "But he did, and the trail of space looped around this boy's essence and puff, he was there. It was only a minute or two before Abernathy reeled him back, but it was long enough for him to give a pretty good description. Of which I was forbidden to say anything about by Dictator Dick. So, keep it quiet." Amry placed her pointer finger over her mouth.

"That's phooey. This Zachary is probably a basket case right now. Top that out with his love for crime and we're better than screwed, we're all next on a long list of victims the Academy will present him with," Sam snapped.

"We don't have a choice." Amry read the pages again. "He was abandoned and treated like dirt."

"The Headmaster picked us for a reason. I'm not happy about this either. But if it could save his soul?" Ophelia's voice trailed off.

"He's not a stray puppy dog, Ophelia. He's gonna cause real trouble for all of us." Sam shoved his chair back. "This is a drag, man."

Ophelia turned away.

"Stop. All of you. Sam, shut up. Lia, turn back around and Bethany, well, you're fine. We don't have a choice. We may not like it, but this is how it is. This guy is going to be here. We do our best to help the Headmaster, end of story. Agreed?" Amry tapped her fingers on the desk. "I said, *agreed*?"

Sam and Bethany mumbled a reluctant yes, and Ophelia half smiled.

"Okay then, I'll go tell them we're ready for tomorrow."

OPHELIA BARELY SLEPT. The trepidation of their new job left her with too many questions to count. She held her head, envisioning the havoc Zachary wreaked when he was alive. A shiver ran down her spine. Well, it felt like where her spine would be if she still had one.

A harsh thump on her dorm room window startled Ophelia into the now. Turning toward the window she saw a barrage of small stones hit the glass. Frowning, she quickly walked over to see who the pitcher was—Sam.

Releasing the latch, she pulled up the window just in time to be a recipient of a second handful of the hard minerals. A larger rock hit her square between the eyes. Wincing, Ophelia cupped the bridge of her nose.

"Ouch! What are you doing, Sam?" Ophelia tried to rub away the pain.

"Sorry. I guess I should have just come up."

"Uh, yeah. That would have been less dangerous for me." Ophelia continued rubbing.

"You okay?" Sam's voice tenuous.

"I'm fine. What do you want?"

"We're all meeting in the library in about thirty minutes. The girls are already there. Amry said she forgot to set the alarm to get you up. She had that early science class."

"So, are you the errand boy?" Ophelia asked, sarcastically.

"No. Well, kind of. I had to go back to my room for something, and you were on the way. I volunteered."

"Okay, you've done your job. I'll be there in a few minutes. First, I need to shower and get dressed." She stuck her tongue out.

"I deserved that. I'll see you there." Sam briskly crossed the lawn.

Ophelia went to the bathroom and turned on the shower. She was the only one of her friends who still maintained the morning ritual. She gazed in the mirror while waiting for the water to steam. Squinting her eyes, she leaned in for a better view. Yup, a knot the size of a nickel angrily sat between her eyes.

Ugh, how do these things keep happening?

A haze of hot mist blurred her reflection, she took the cue and stepped into the box of steam. Standing under the rain of comfort, her body relaxed as she soaked in the peace. She had a feeling this would be the only quiet for a while. Life at the Academy was about to get a whole new meaning.

After a few minutes of bliss, she turned off the water and toweled off. Another aspect of the living she could leave behind, and yet, something kept drawing her in to perform even the most mundane tasks of the life she once knew. When she was ready, she opted for a stroll instead of gliding. It took a few minutes longer, but she enjoyed basking in the sunshine.

Ophelia rounded the corner of the library and slid through the honey oak doors. Her friends were seated at one of the many rectangular tables in the center of the room. Surrounded on all four sides by books dating back to the twelfth century, Ophelia stood for a moment taking in the aroma. It tickled her nostrils and surrounded her mind with exhilaration. She was the sponge to the waterfall of knowledge contained in this room. Its sole purpose to deliver pleasure to her waiting senses.

"Over here. What are you doing?" Amry smiled.

"Just taking it all in." Ophelia sat.

"Honestly, you make me laugh. You're here just about every day of the week and it still excites you."

"Yup. There's so much to learn. The information is practically endless. Why, don't you feel like that?"

"Well, sure. I like coming here, but it doesn't quite affect me the same way. Are you okay today?"

"Sure. Why wouldn't I be?" Ophelia's eyes widened.

"You weren't yourself yesterday. I mean you were, but extra stressed. Sort of mousy. I barely heard you utter a word all day. Was it because we were called into the Headmaster's office?"

"No. It wasn't the highlight of my day. You know I hate dealing with adults, but that wasn't it." Ophelia looked away.

"What then?" Amry reached out and patted Ophelia's hand.

"It was my anniversary." Ophelia's voice shook.

"Oh. I'm so sorry. I forgot. No wonder you were a bundle of nerves."

"It's okay. It's over, and time to move on."

"Hey, what happened to your face?' Amry reached out but Ophelia quickly retracted.

"Don't. The damn thing is throbbing. Sam thought it would be a good idea to throw rocks at my window." Ophelia's eyes narrowed.

"Sam, you're an idiot." Amry glared at him.

"What? It was an accident. I told her I was sorry."

"He did." Bethany chimed in.

"Can we get on with this? Zachary gets here in twenty minutes." Ophelia glanced at the antique clock on the wall. "We don't interact, just observe. If any one of us sees Zachary acting strange or doing something he shouldn't, we report it immediately to the Headmaster, right?"

Ophelia trembled as a cool breeze swept across the base of the neck. She shivered. Whipping her head around, a shadow danced across the glass of the large rectangular window toward the back of the room.

"Did you see that?" Ophelia whispered.

"What?" Amry leaned in.

"That shadow? It was right behind us."

"I didn't see anything, but we better get it together. It's almost time." Amry nervously tapped her foot.

"I think he's here." Ophelia pointed at the door.

Everyone in the room stopped what they were reading to look up. The air carried a feeling of discontent that wrapped itself around the room squeezing out every drop of pleasure.

Mr. Coal and Mr. Rain wedged the male teen between them, escorting him to the information desk.

Zachary's lanky frame towered over the khaki twins. Mr. Rain and Mr. Coal didn't seem to notice. They had a firm grip on each of his arms, establishing who was in charge. His tousled brown hair and grey skin were the frame for his crystal blue eyes.

Ophelia tightened the hold on her stomach, leaning forward just enough to soothe the pain. Her anxiety had gone from ten to a hundred in the past twenty seconds.

Zachary scanned the room and stopped when his gaze met Amry. Not the type of girl to back down, she locked his stare with her own. Neither blinked. A maniacal curl of the lip almost led to words vomiting out of his mouth, but Mr. Rain tugged firmly on his arm, knocking Zachary slightly off balance and breaking his link with Amry.

Ophelia let out a long shaky breath. Remaining in solid form took a good portion of their energy. They had agreed to try and remain as opaque as possible, to appear strong. But it took its toll and Ophelia wavered, her celestial uttered like ripples in the water.

"It's quite all right, you're dead. Let it go, my dear," A gruff voice scraped her ears.

Ophelia jumped. *I guess Mr. Rain's grip wasn't as tight as he thought.*

"Miss. The tiny one. Did you hear me?"

Zachary's words disturbed her. Like a knife, they pierced through her ghostly shell and ripped open the cavity where her heart once was, bringing back the memories of death. It had been so long since she had seen her family. Her mother and father must have been inconsolable the day she and Haven started their beginning.

It was spring, her favorite season. The trees were growing fat with new, lush green leaves, and flowers bloomed the most brilliant hues of pink, purple and yellow. The air transitioned from an early chill to a mid- morning warmth that was perfect for tea and toast on the sun-drenched porch. Her mother had asked if she would watch Haven for a few hours while both parents did some shopping in town. The following week, her little sister would turn eight and they wanted to surprise her. They were picking up a brand-new dollhouse that her dad had ordered from England.

Ophelia didn't mind. She liked spending time with her. As siblings go, they were close. Maybe it was the large span of years between them, Ophelia felt more like an aunt than a big sister. Whatever the reason, it was ne with her.

Their parents had been gone for about an hour, and Haven was playing in the front yard. Ophelia had nestled into a rocker on the porch and was reading one of her favorite books, *Molly Make-Believe* by Eleanor Hallowell Abbott. Rarely did a motor car come down their street, but they had been instructed by their father to stay away when it did. Ophelia set her book on a side table when she heard the honking of a horn in the distance. Standing to see which direction it was coming from, she noticed Haven running out into the road to retrieve a ball that had gotten away.

Ophelia bolted down the five steps and across the lawn in time to see the car coming from the right, and her sister facing the other way. Without a thought, she ran into the middle of the road and wrapped her arms around Haven, before hearing a dissonant thud. When she woke up, her sister was running toward a man standing at the end of the block. She screamed for her to come back, but it was too late. He and Haven were gone.

Through the years she was able to find out the man was a Soul Gatherer. He takes the newly deceased when their spirits are confused and lures them with hope. He especially likes the innocence of children. No one is sure where he keeps them, but a few have been able to escape. Most of them adults. Once they leave, all their knowledge of his location fades away.

Perhaps he can cast a powerful spell, no one is sure. What they can remember is unending sadness. Ophelia surmised he must be lost himself. Protectors, like Mr. Coal and Mr. Rain, have tried through the years to find his hidden sanctuary, but each time they get close, he manages to cloak his secret once again. The light had come for her several times over the past one hundred years, and it will keep coming, until she finds Haven.

She glared back at Zachary, who was being led out of the library. A sigh of relief escaped her lips. He was going to be trouble.

ALEX MCKENNA CAUGHT himself as his chin slid down his left hand. Nodding off in class was beginning to be a habit. The past few weeks after the Geranium murders had been rough on sleep. Playing the vision of losing Tom Kirkpatrick to the dark spirit over and over in his head left little time to relax. It was his self-appointed restitution for his part in Tom's demise. Alex glanced out of one of the large rectangular windows in the classroom. The grey, dingy shadow looming over the parking lot was not the scenic view Alex had expected. But his math class faced east, the stunning asphalt view was its reward. As his glare intensified, the black top of the ground below mesmerized him. Lulling his tired body into a light trance. He hadn't noticed the sudden drop in temperature surrounding him, until a gust of cold air graced the nape of his neck.

Twitching, it sent shivers down his vertebrae. From the corner of his right eye, a shadow danced across the room. Alex whipped his head around; the air was still. *Was this his mind screaming desperately for sleep, or was there something here?* He inhaled a deep breath through his nose and exhaled through his mouth to calm his senses. Nothing. *He just might be going crazy from lack of REM sleep.*

Popping a breath freshener in his mouth, he prayed the minty freshness would keep sleep at bay.

GHOSTS TAKE A SHOWER

Ophelia shot up, tossing her fluffy down comforter aside, it draped to the floor. A ripple of fear stroked her ghostly spine and she shuddered. Padding her feet on the cherry wood floor, the cold cut through them like a knife. What was happening to her? She tried to cast off her latest dream, but she couldn't. Haven was out there somewhere, waiting for her to come. Normally her visions were safe. Haven playing with her toys, Ophelia teaching her how to ride a bike, fun things. But this time it was different. A black haze surrounded the little girl, closing in, it covered her tiny body until there was nothing left.

Days like this were the hardest. The guilt surrounding Haven's abduction overwhelmed her. She brought her hands to her head and squeezed, the vice grip did little to alleviate the pressure that was building like a geyser in her brain. If she were like everyone else, sleep would alleviate the pain she felt. But she wasn't. It wasn't clear why she still felt the warmth of the sun, or the simple pleasure of a shower each morning. No one else in the Academy still had human ties to life like she did. Her friends tried to understand. Amry, her best friend, did better than most. However, *people often fear what they don't understand.* That was something her father used to say.

She decided to take a trip to see the resident healer at the Academy. Dominique Dunworthy had started her beginning about a year ago. Transitioning between the living and the ever after, her soul was sent to the Academy to wait. Being a trained psychiatrist, the council thought it would be wise to use her skills for some of the younger souls that were having difficulty.

Ms. Dunworthy had a small office on the other side of campus behind the library. Normally an appointment was preferred, but Ms. Dunworthy often made an exception for Ophelia. Considering her strange ties with the living world, the doctor was both intrigued and concerned, therefore she gave Ophelia an open-door policy.

Normally she would wait, but this morning her insides were twisted in knots. This dream was too much to handle on her own, she needed help.

Three knocks on the red door gained entrance to the one person equipped to answer Ophelia's questions.

"Good morning, Ophelia, come, sit down. You caught me at just the right time. I don't have another appointment for thirty minutes. How are you doing?"

Ms. Dunworthy sat in a large black leather chair that swiveled when she pushed the ground with her feet. Her blonde hair lay loose, cascading over the top of her shoulders, and gold rim glasses surrounded her soft brown, almond shaped eyes. Insisting on a white lab coat when she met her beginning, the staff conceded because she was a doctor. Normally, no one got a choice. You're given an outfit from the time you lived in. They say it helps to keep a newly transitioned soul more comfortable.

A well-kept secret, everyone arrives in their birthday suit. "I'm okay. Not really. I had a dream last night that really upset me." Ophelia fidgeted with the hem of her dress.

"Hmm. I'm still getting used to hearing you say that," Ms. Dunworthy said gently.

"What?" Ophelia cocked her head.

"You were dreaming. One day we're going to figure that out. For now, though, let's address what's upsetting you. Tell me about the dream."

"I see Haven. At first, she's smiling and happy. The sun is shining and there's a golden glow surrounding her. But something startles her, she twitches, and the darkness begins to devour the light. Inch by inch it crawls closer to her. She collapses on the ground and draws her knees to her chest. Then she tucks her head down, not looking at the shadows that are about to swallow her. She yells out a name, *Alex!* And then she's gone. The blackness takes her."

Ophelia waited for a response, but Ms. Dunworthy just sat for a moment with her eyes narrowed, and back stiff. When she finally spoke, the explanation frightened Ophelia more than the dream.

"Did either of you know anyone by that name in life?" The doctor leaned forward.

"No. Why do you ask?" Ophelia squirmed in her chair.

"I don't believe this was a dream. I believe your sister was reaching out."

"Why do you say that?"

"The name. If you had both known an Alex in life, I'd say coincidence perhaps. But you didn't. Therefore, I think this is someone Haven wants you to know about, or maybe it's the name of the man holding her. Either way, I strongly believe she is attempting communication."

Ophelia's brow furrowed. This was not the explanations she'd expected.

"What can I do? I've tried every avenue I know to find her, but I have nothing." Ophelia quaked inside.

"Wait and see if she comes to you again, but this time, try

communicating with her. Be aware of yourself in the vision. She's searching for you, but you're the beacon. That gives you more control than you realize. Try to find out who Alex is."

Ms. Dunworthy stood and walked over to Ophelia. She bent down and gently squeezed her hand.

"You will find her. I feel it. Pay attention Ophelia, the answers are there if you let them in."

Ophelia forced a smile before getting up and thanking the doctor for her help. Floating back to her dorm room, she trembled from the unsettling weight in her chest. Something told her she was running out of time.

AMRY WAS LYING on her bed when Ophelia got home. She was quiet, avoided her usual greeting as Ophelia closed the door. Another, less pressing issue than Haven's whereabouts was Amry's change in personality the past week. Normally, Amry was, well—Amry. Smiles and happiness were a daily outfit, but Ophelia wondered what was really going on inside, when the glee turned to gloom. Amry had taken an interest in a junior, Jeffrey Wright. They started spending nights together in the courtyard just outside Ophelia and Amry's dorm window. But without warning one evening, just after they kissed goodnight, Jeffrey took the light. Amry was stunned. She never mentioned a word about him again. Ophelia tried to gently coax her friend to confide in her what might have happened, but it was useless.

"I didn't think you'd be here. Don't you have that group thing for science?" Ophelia swirled around the room searching for her notebook.

"It got canceled." Amry pulled the pillow over her head. "Oh. That's too bad. Why did it get canceled?'

"I canceled it," her voice muffled.

"You? Why?" Ophelia sat next to her friend.

"Because I wanted to. End of story. What were you doing out so early?"

"I went to see Ms. Dunworthy."

"Why? What's wrong?'

"Bad dreams." Ophelia floated to her own bed.

"About?" Amry rolled over.

"I'll tell, if you will." Ophelia narrowed her eyes.

"Tell what?" Amry snapped.

"Why you think Jeffrey left."

"I don't know."

"Yes, you do."

Amry glided up toward the ceiling and disappeared. In moments, she walked through the front door and plopped down on her bed. She held a letter in her hand.

"Where did you go? And what's that?" Ophelia stretched her neck to get a better look.

"My locker. This was waiting for me the morning after Jeffey left.

Amry,

I don't think I could ever express how much you mean to me. If we had been lucky enough to know each other during our breather years, I know I would have wanted to spend every minute with you. But the light has come for me several times lately, and I have you to thank for that. Never being in love was my burden. It stopped me from moving on and reuniting with my family. I know you'll never leave if Ophelia is still searching for Haven. I get it, I really do. You're as good a friend as you are a lover, but it's my time and I didn't want to give you added pressure. I know you would have refused, and this way is easier for both of us. I hope one day you can forgive me.

Eternally yours,

Jeffrey

Amry let the letter fall from her fingers and float to the

floor. "What the skilamalink? How did he get it in your locker if he was already gone?" Ophelia gritted her teeth.

"He asked his friend Oliver to put it there after the light came for him again." Amry pulled the comforter up to her neck and folded into a fetus pose. "I thought getting a scoundrel like Zachary Kowal at the Academy might take my mind off of it. I tried to push it down deep, keep up the smiles, but yesterday Oliver approached me after the last class. Told me how much Jeffrey really did love me, how it was so hard for him. If it was so damn hard, then why did he go?" Amry's voice was shaky.

"I wish I knew. I'll never understand boys." Ophelia bit her lower lip. "They do the strangest things.'

"Your turn." Amry sat up. "Spill. What's going on?"

Ophelia explained her recent dream about Haven, the name Alex, and Ms. Dunworthy's interpretation.

"Visions, huh. Do you think she's right?" Amry snapped the letter up from the floor and place it under her pillow.

"I don't know, but I'm going to try out her advice. It can't hurt. There's something else, though."

"What's that?"

"I got a feeling like Haven's running out of time." Ophelia glanced out the window. The clouds rolling in soaked up the last drop of sunlight, casting a dark silhouette in the courtyard. "I need to find out who this Alex is, and what he means to Haven.

MEET HAVEN

The house was peaceful, Alex's mom and brother were sleeping. They were leaving early in the morning for a week in Orlando, Florida. Visiting family who had migrated to warmer climate, was a yearly trip he'd have to miss this time. It was mid-year finals at the Academy, so he would have to experience palm trees and sandy beaches second hand. Checking his phone for the time, it was later than he thought. He ambled into the kitchen and rummaged through the refrigerator for leftovers. Pizza, orange chicken, and a three-day old cheeseburger from Grille Kings—pizza it was. Throwing a slice of pie on a paper plate, and nuking it for sixty seconds, answered the gnawing pangs in his stomach. A glass of cola and he was off to bed.

A soothing shower called to him as he rounded the corner to the second floor. Not bothering to retrieve his pajamas, he swung directly into the bathroom. A thick, midnight blue robe hung from a hook behind the door. He had given his mom grief for buying him such a lame gift, but he used it way more often than he'd admit to her. Twisting the shower faucet on hot, he let steam build up in the room, warming his bones.

Removing his shirt, he yanked on his binder, twisting it down past his hips until it dropped to the floor. His chest sawed a heavy breath as the air hit his bare skin. It felt good to be free of the day's constraints. Turning to check his five o'clock shadow in the foggy mirror, he reached out and wiped away the condensation. Glancing down at the exposed fleshy plumps protruding from his chest, his stomach roiled. He was running out of patience, surgery needed to happen sooner rather than later.

Stepping under the hot rain, he tilted back his head and let the water wash away the memories that suffocated his mind. Learning to let go of the death of an innocent was harder than anything he'd ever done. It wasn't working.

Jolted by the picture of Tom's dead body lying in his living room, Alex huddled by the wall of the shower. Looking down at his trembling hands, the pruned tips of his fingers beckoned for him to get out. He had lost track of time. Soaping down, he quickly rinsed and shut down the tranquility. Reaching for the towel that he had thrown on the lid of the toilet, he briskly dried his body and wrapped up. A chill tickled the back of his neck and he shuddered. From the corner of his eye, the ash of a bright light poked his temple with the same precision as an ice pick. Alex grabbed the side of his head and squeezed. Tilting his chin down, he momentarily lost his balance. The vision beside him spiraled with a kaleidoscope of luminous shades of green. Slowly, the ribbon of color etched out to form an opening in the center. The eye of the storm.

Alex squinted, straining to focus on the anomaly. Reaching out, he caught a glimpse of the goosebumps mapping their way over the skin of his forearm. He recoiled his hand to his side. *What the hell am I doing?* Stepping away, he pressed his back against the door and faced his unwanted guest. In the heart of the calm stood a little girl. Her chestnut braid cascaded down the front of her long white nightgown, masking portions of the pale blue lace trim. Soft brown eyes held the weight of sadness. Both arms stretched out, fully extended, her small hands trying to wriggle closer to him. The child's mouth mimicked the mechanics of conversation, but only silence escaped her pale, pink lips.

"Who are you?" Alex whispered.

The little girl's words fell silent.

"I can't hear you. Can you understand me? If you can, nod your head."

The child nodded yes.

"Are you lost?" Alex inched closer.

Placing her arms by her side, she nodded again.

"Are you in danger?"

Her head turned away.

Alex's shoulder's stiffened *Not a yes, but not a no either.* "Are you trying to find someone?"

The girl's mouth moved, her lips forming a long trail of silent sentences.

"Whoa. Stop. I still can't hear you." Alex furrowed his brow.

The little girl put her hands up, covering her face.

"Hey, it's okay. I'll figure something out, hold on."

Alex sized up the room looking for anything to aid in their communication. Staring at the half-fogged mirror, his eyes widened. Hastily, he turned the shower back on and twisted the knob until it rested solely on the hot water. Within moments the air thickened and a veil of steam covered the reflective glass. With his pointer finger, he laid out the alphabet across the balmy surface. Turning back toward the child, she was smiling.

"You understand?" Alex pointed to the letters.

Clapping her hands, she nodded yes.

"Okay. I'll ask you a question and then starting with A, I'll point to the letters. You nod to let me know if it's the right one. Good?"

Rapidly, she agreed.

"Let's start with something simple. What's your name?"

Alex pointed to the letters one at a time until he hit H. The girl drew up a hand to indicate stop.

"Okay great. Now let's go to the vowels. A?"

She nodded yes.

Once again, he started pointing. When he reached V, she jumped up.

"Let's see we have, H—a—v ... huh. I'm not sure, let's keep going. It's probably another vowel. How about, I?"

She adamantly shook her head no.

"E?" Alex outlined the letters on the bottom corner of the mirror.

She clapped once again.

"H—A—V—E... Haven? Is that it? Are you Haven?" The girl grinned and patted both hands on her chest. "Nice to meet you, Haven. I'm Alex."

The little girl pointed to her eye. "Something's wrong with your eyes?"

She closed her eyes and shook her head. First pointing to her eyes again, she then pointed to him.

"Eye? Eye—or wait, I? Haven is it I?" Alex tapped the letter in the alphabet string.

She replied with a nod and pointed to Alex again.

"Hmm. What are you trying to say? I, me, I, Alex, I'm Alex! Haven, you already know who I am?"

Haven nodded her head in agreement.

"Did you know me before you died? How do you know me?" Alex fired the questions like bullets.

Without warning, Haven's face dropped, and her body stiffened. Snapping her gaze to peer over her shoulder, she turned back to Alex, wide-eyed and gaping mouth—she was screaming.

"Haven. What's wrong? Haven!"

Before the last syllable escaped his breath, she was gone. Stunned, Alex furiously retraced the last few minutes in his mind, hoping to find something he might have missed.

Nothing. Frustrated, he ambled to his bedroom and pulled on some sweats and a T-shirt. Turning back the covers, he slid underneath the solace of warm blankets and feathery-like pillow. Reaching for his phone from the table beside his bed, he called the one person that always made him feel better, Margaret.

She picked it up after the first ring.

"Hey, I thought you were going to bed after I left?"

Margaret's voice soothed Alex's tension.

"I decided to take a hot shower. Tesoro, something happened," Alex's voice cracked.

"What? Are you all right?"

"I'm fine. A little off balance. This young girl, Haven, came to me. She couldn't be more than seven or eight. It was strange. She spoke, but there was no sound. It was like watching a damn silent film," Alex sighed.

"How do you know her name then?"

"It was crazy. The room was steamy, so I wrote the alphabet on the mirror. I felt like I was in a Wheel of Fortune nightmare. She was smart though, caught on right away."

"What did she want?" Margaret cleared her throat.

"That's it, I don't know. One minute we're having a conversation, and the next she gets this horrified look in her eyes, and she's gone. I think she was screaming. I don't know what to do. I have no idea who she is, or where she came from. Just this overwhelming sense of needing to help her. I think she really needs me."

"Maybe tomorrow you should call your Gram. She might be able to give you some ideas."

"Yeah. I'll try her in the morning. She's probably gone to bed, which is what I'm gonna try and do. You still working on homework?"

"I am. A couple more minutes and I'm done. My eyes can barely stay open. I'll see you at school tomorrow," Margaret's voice trailed off.

Alex set his phone down on the table.

Rolling over to face the wall, he traced the encounter with Haven in his mind. Frame by frame—until sleep ushered in the darkness

AT THE BREAK of dawn his phone alarm sounded, and Alex fumbled to shut it. A restless night focused on dreams of Haven left him feeling exhausted. *Thank the gods it's Friday*, he thought. Throwing back the security of his comforter, he rolled out of bed. Retracting his feet from the bite of the cold floor, he hesitated before releasing them again and hobbling to his dresser. Pulling out a pair of white crew socks, he quickly put them on. Better. His hunger churned the acids in his stomach, echoing a loud grumble.

Breakfast before a shower sounded like a good plan. Ambling down the stairs, he grinned. There was a loud commotion of voices coming from the kitchen—his aunts had arrived. Jennie and Carla were his moms' older sisters, and the three of them were glued at the hip.

He could hear his little brother, Wilby, begging to sit in the front seat of the car, and his mom issuing a firm no. Walking through the gateway to chaos, he was greeted by his exasperated mom.

"Alex, there you are, I thought I was going to have to come

up and get you." His mom continued to pack a small cooler with water. "We're heading out, and we should be at your uncle's house in two days. Tonight, we're stopping in Jacksonville, the hotel information is on the fridge."

"You guys all cramming in one car?" asked Alex.

His aunts were piling luggage in their arms, they looked like they were evacuating a sinking ship.

"Of course, mia prezioso," Aunt Jennie continued, "it would not be safe to split the family. What if there's an accident? Or one of us gets lost? We stay together."

"That's right," Aunt Carla interjected, "we're always stronger as a family."

Alex understood. They were stronger together, much like any other family, but they also shared a special bond—their abilities. As one, they could do some awesome things, but as a group, they were nearly unstoppable.

"Mio figlio, stay out of trouble while we're gone. You hear me? No new cases. Gram is still in town if you need anything. But take this time to rest, we all suffered a huge loss, and the wounds have only begun to heal. I wish you were going with us, I'd feel much better," said his mom.

"Ma. I'll be fine. Margaret and I are gonna study, and we have some movie time planned. It's all good. Don't worry about me, okay?"

"Come here." His mom squeezed him tight.

"Gina let's go. We'll hit a load of traffic if we leave any later." Aunt Jennie huffed. "Alex, listen to what your mom said, no funny business."

Alex nodded, he knew nothing he would say was going to satisfy their worry, he'd just have to hold on a few more minutes until they left. After an eternity of kisses, and hugs exchanged between *everybody,* the front door slammed shut.

He took a moment to soak in the calm, it felt peaceful. Perusing the kitchen for the ingredients to stunt the growing hunger in his belly, his go to breakfast of toasted crusty bread, smothered in butter, would have to wait. He'd forgotten to stop by the deli on the way home from school yesterday. The coffee was ready, *thank you technology,* and after a few minutes of indecision, he decided Stella D'oro original breakfast cookies, would be the best substitution. Perfect for dunking, his taste buds salivated thinking of the sugary substance.

Setting a plate with four cookies and a mug of coffee on the table, he called his grandmother and put it on speaker.

"Bonzetta. You're calling early, are you all right?"

"I'm fine, Gram. I had a visitor last night and I'm not sure what to do."

Alex detailed the story about Haven, and the bad feeling that was haunting him.

"You want to call her spirit back?"

"Yes. I think she really needs me. It's bugging me that I can't hear her. That's a first."

"It might be where the child is located. There are places that can keep a soul from finding the light. Realms beyond the space of the living and the dead. Do you remember that boy your grandfather helped in Naples last year? The one that haunted him for months. He was one of those souls. Not with the living or the dead, he wandered between worlds, held captive by a lost spirit. It drained your papa trying to track him down. The spirit kept moving the boy to different dimensions."

"How do I do this, find out where she is?" Alex bit a cookie.

"If this girl truly needs your help, she will find a way to contact you again. When she does, get as much information as you can. Anything she can give you will help."

"Can't we just summon her like we did Catherine?" Alex questioned.

Catherine was a tormented spirit forced to kill by the

human hand of Greta Kirkpatrick, a woman with an eighty-year grudge. She possessed a hold on Catherine's soul using dark magic.

"No. When a soul is trapped in the between world, summoning spells can be inaccurate. We might cause the child to wind up some place worse than she's in already."

"Okay. I'll wait. I guess I don't have a choice." Alex put his phone down and shoved it.

Frustration was not an emotion he dealt with well.

***

The bus ride to school was quick. Lost in his thoughts of Haven, he barely noticed Heather Johnson, the spirit of a young girl killed by a hit and run fifteen years ago. Every day she rode the bus from her parent's former house to school. Alex tried to help her cross over a few times, but she wasn't ready. Normally, he'd give her a nod when he boarded the bus, but not today. The ghost must have missed the attention, because for the first time in two years, she sat next to him. Alex didn't notice until the bumps mapped their way across his forearms. His *spidey sense,* the terminology Margaret coined his psychic ability and his family referred to as their *know,* had kicked into high gear. The closer a spirit was to him, the more predominant the bumps. He rubbed his forearms and pivoted his head to face the filtered spirit of Heather. When an entity uses its energy to appear corporal, it drains them. So, most of the time, they remain in a celestial state. Their bodies muted in color, roll through the air like ripples in water. Alex smiled and Heather was satisfied. Drifting back to her usual seat, she went back to her normal ritual of staring out the window.

The bus stopped at its destination, The Academy of Cain Amry Thearige. A long name for the man that had the original school built in England, several hundred years ago. His great grandson insisted on carrying the name over when he donated a small fortune for the American version. That was over a hundred years ago, and Alex wondered why they just didn't simplify it for modern society. It was a cool name but try letting that roll off your tongue when you're in a hurry. The kids just referred to it as the Academy. It worked.

Margaret was waiting for him in their usual spot by the bleachers.

"Hey you." Alex wrapped his arms around her waist and tasted a sweet chocolate cherry kiss.

"You look tired." she ran her fingers through his hair.

"I'm beat. Had another bad night. Only this time Haven took over where Tom left off."

"You speak to your gram?" She sat.

"Yup. I gotta wait until Haven comes back. If she comes back." He frowned.

"If she needs help like you think, she'll find a way." Margaret gently raised the corner of her mouth.

A deafening ring signaled the start of the school day. Alex groaned before caressing Margaret's lips with his. They were headed in opposite directions, and he hated leaving her. Holding onto her hand as her fingers slipped through his, he squeezed gently before letting go.

Begrudgingly stepping one foot in front of the other, he landed in front of Chemistry, his least favorite class.

Luckily, he had a seat by the window, and unlike Math, this one faced the west side of the building. He could see the three-block strip of town in the distance, and below, the grassy fields that lead to the bleachers. A much better view than asphalt. Taking out the book, *Chemistry in the Community,* he opened to the assigned reading and let his mind wander. Dust particles danced along a luminous beam of yellow ribbon, punching its way through the glass. Mesmerized, Alex swayed with the swirling motion. A flush of cold air wisped around the base of his neck brushing up the tiny hairs, his hands trembled, and the room slowly spun with the speed of a child's ride at Disney World.

Glancing around the room, the peculiarity was his alone. The other students had their attention on the assigned class work. Alex's gaze focused on the corner of the wall behind the teacher's desk. Peeling back like wallpaper, the landscape of the classroom began to change, replacing the sleek, modern desks with thick, solid wood chairs and tables. A fireplace in the corner crackled, illuminating the room. Heavy drapes covered most of the windows, drawn back in the corners with gold tassels. The clanging of a bell startled him, and he nearly jumped from his seat. Checking with the kids next to him, no one seemed to notice. The door to the class flew open, and the students glided in. The waves of their celestial bodies sliced through the air and took a seat. Alex leaned forward, *could they see him?* He thought. Trying not to attract too much attention from the present-day teens surrounding him, he knocked one of his books on the floor to see if the ghostly class responded. One girl looked up. She turned around and locked eyes with Alex.

"Who are you?" The girl rose from her seat.

Hovering, she reached out and then pulled back.

"Ophelia. What the hell are you doing?" Sam quipped.

"Don't you see him?" Ophelia's eyes widened.

"Who?" Sam looked around the class.

"Him. Right there in front of me." Ophelia pointed.

Alex was stunned. Not by the meeting with the dead teens, he was used to that. When you see the departed for as long as you can remember, it becomes *normal*. No, he was shocked by the resemblance the girl had to Haven. Same eyes, hair color and delicate features. Only this girl was clearly several years older.

"I don't see anyone. Dang it, you okay, Ophelia?" Sam's voice softened.

Ophelia didn't respond. Fixated on Alex, she asked again.

"Who are you?" She inched closer.

"A ..."

"Mr. McKenna, do you mind?" Mrs. Jenkins said sharply. Startled, Alex gasped when he realized he had unknowingly migrated toward the front of the class. He was standing at Mrs. Jenkins' desk, facing the dry erase board. Scanning the room for remnants of the ghostly girl, he sighed. There was nothing left of his vision but embarrassment. Head down, he murmured an apology to the teacher, and shuffled back to his desk.

"Way to go McKenna. As if you weren't already weird enough." A voice echoed from behind.

Alex didn't need to turn around to know where it was coming from. Kyle Branders was the school bully who had been giving him crap since he first arrived at the Academy. Ignoring him was hard but feeding into him would be worse.

Closing his eyes, he retreated into the event that had captivated him moments ago. *Who was she? Why did she remind him of Haven? And how did they connect?* The barrage of questions hammering around in his brain gave Alex a headache. Balancing his chin under his folded hands, he tried to calm the neurons and ease the pain.

Jolted by the firm grip of someone shaking his shoulder, Alex looked up. The class was empty, and Mrs. Jenkins was standing over him with pursed lips. Glancing up at the clock, it was eight-thirty. He had slept through the entire period.

THE EMBITTERED ZACHARY KNOWLES

Ophelia slid back into her chair.

"Hey what's going on? You sure you're okay? That was some pretty far out crap." Sam rolled his eyes.

"I saw this—boy. He was about our age, but I think it was the living world. He wasn't like us."

"Did he say anything to you?"

"No. He was about to, but something stopped him, and he disappeared." Ophelia looked away. "I don't understand what's happening."

"What do you mean?" Sam whispered.

"Well, today I see this boy and the other night ... never mind. I know this stuff creeps you out." Ophelia looked down at her desk.

"No. Lia, it's okay. I want to hear," Sam said confidentially. Ophelia was stunned. Sam never wanted to know about her connection to the living, and he never, ever called her Lia. Only Amry referred to her like that.

"Why? You usually go out of your way to avoid listening to me when it's about things like this."

"I know, I'm sorry. It made me uncomfortable in the past.

But not for the reasons you think. I'm a little jealous. You still get to do the things I wish I could, but I'm done with that. From now on, keep on truckin'." Sam grinned.

"Where did this change of heart come from?" Ophelia leaned in closer to him.

"Zachary."

"How did Zachary change your mind?"

"Reading about his life, what he went through as a breather and then after his beginning, it made me think. The guy has basically been alone his whole life and after life. Yeah, the Headmaster is his uncle, but clearly, he hasn't had much to do with the guy's world. My life before this was pretty good with friends and family, but when I got here, it was a strange experience. If I didn't have you nerds, I ... never mind, I don't want to think about it. Anyway, understand?' Sam winked.

She did. Ophelia was lost for so long and if it weren't for Amry, she still would be.

"The other night I had a dream about Haven. It was a bad one, she was in trouble. She yelled out a name—Alex. I spoke to Ms. Dunworthy, she thinks it's Haven communicating with me."

"Oh wow. This is the first time this has happened, right?" "Yes. The doctor also said that either it's someone who can

help us, or maybe the person holding her. But I don't know, that doesn't feel right to me." Ophelia slumped down in her chair.

"What do you think it means?"

"I think Haven is trying to give me the name of someone who can help. The thing is though, how would she know this? I mean the Soul Gatherer has had her hidden since the first day of her beginning."

"Maybe one of the other souls who escaped knew of someone who could help and told her about him before they got away." Sam nodded and grinned.

"You're pretty pleased with yourself. What are you a detective now?" Ophelia giggled.

"To the max," Sam said in a cocky voice.

"And there he is, the Sam Burkletter we all know and love." Sam turned around and Ophelia spent the rest of the class period fixated on the boy in her vision. *But it wasn't a vision, was it?* she thought.

After class, she and Sam met Amry and Bethany at what they all laughingly referred to as the cafeteria. A large building with tables, chairs, and a kitchen. No one understood why it was there. Clearly no student attending The Academy of Souls yearned for a quick lunch before afternoon classes.

"You ever wonder why we have showers? I mean aside from Ophelia, they're pointless. Like this building," Bethany blurted out. "I used to love to sing in the shower, though."

"It must be crazy in that head of yours, Bethany. You're always popping off with the most random thoughts." Amry chuckled. "What did you like to sing? Did you have a favorite song or group?"

"Ohhh, for me it was David Cassidy all the way. He was so cute. I did like the Bee Gees too. But they weren't like David." Bethany batted her lashes.

"I was more of a Rolling Stones and Jethro Tull fan, but I can dig what you mean. Mick Jagger did it for me. It was funny, my mom thought he was ugly, but not me, he was gorgeous. I even had tongue patches on my jeans, mom hated it." Amry laughed.

Bethany's voice softened. "My dad used to tease me about it." She smiled. "I had posters of David all over my walls. I knew it frustrated him because the scotch tape marred the paint. But he never said anything negative about it to me. In fact, he'd sometimes give me a couple of bucks to get the latest issue of Tiger Beat. David was always on the cover. I miss my dad." Her smile faded.

"Was he still alive when you started your beginning?" Sam stroked her hair.

"He was. Might probably still be. Although he'd be very old by now. That was nearly forty years ago. It sounds so strange to say that. You'd think I'd be used to all this by now. But I don't know, does anyone ever really get used to it?"

"I myself enjoy being dead." A deep voice carried from across the room.

The four of them turned around and cringed. Zachary Kowal was standing in front of the door.

"What in tarnation?" Ophelia murmured.

"Well we're supposed to be watching him. This is kind of convenient," Sam said.

"I don't care if it's convenient, the guy gives me the creeps." Bethany scooted closer to her boyfriend.

"I'm with her, he's creepy times ten." Amry turned away and locked eyes with Ophelia.

"You understand I can hear every word, do you not?" Zachary moved closer.

The group closed in their circle, leaving no room for the unwanted boy.

"Whatever, we don't care. Are you following us?" Sam puffed his chest.

"Now why would I want to subject myself to such a torturous way to pass the time? I am merely wandering about, assessing the lay of the land."

"I thought Mr. Coal and Mr. Rain were keeping an eye on you?" Ophelia squeaked.

"Oh, what do you know. It's the freak. No. They were with me for a time, but they cannot watch me all the time. There is really nothing they could do if I wanted to start something. They are just a pair of low-level reject sorcerers. The guys I run with would obliterate them." Zachary tapped his lips with his fingers.

"Why don't you go? There's nothing going on here that could possibly interest you." Amry broke the circle and faced Zachary.

"You are the pretty one. I heard about you… Too bad you are closed up tight like a clam shell." Zachary sneered.

"Hey! Don't talk to her like that." Sam snapped.

"It's okay Sam, I got this." Amry grinned.

"Big tough boy. You're so full of shit. The only reason you're not in *The Nowhere* right now is because of the Headmaster. You had blood on your side. You think because you were a minuscule, microfiber of a thug when you were still a breather, it carries some weight here? We're not afraid of you, we said you creep us out. Kind of like when you see a cat with two heads. You're an oddity, something for us to gawk at." Amry whipped up toward the ceiling and landed in front of Zachary. "You're right though, our job is to spy on you. No sense in pretending if you already heard us. But remember, us spying on you means we have all the power." Amry flicked him on the side of the head.

"You are delusional." Zachary cackled.

"Am I? All we gotta do is go to the Headmaster and tell him about all the horrible things you're doing. Then it's bye-bye, Zachary. I wonder if *The Nowhere* is as dark and cold as they say it is? Don't piss us off, thug. Or else you'll be finding out real soon." Ophelia was beyond stunned. Amry was always a kind, warm soul. This Amry just cut Zachary off below the knees, andthen stuffed the rest of his body in a garbage can. Figuratively speaking. But badass.

"The pretty one has more to her than just a face. I like it." Zachary sneered. "I will go, but it is not because of you." Zachary glared at Ophelia. "This one is crazy beyond any help my uncle or anyone here can give her. I saw you."

"You saw what?" Amry stepped in front of Ophelia.

"I saw her in class. She conversed with someone who was

not there, seeing things that are only in her deranged head. I don't want to be any closer than I have to."

Amry smirked. "So, you're afraid of a small girl? You're pathetic."

Zachary raised his fist but then abruptly stopped. Turning around, he left in silence.

"What the hell was that?" Bethany exclaimed.

"Forget that. Who the heck are you?" Ophelia looked at Amry.

"Right? Where did that attitude come from?" Sam ran his fingers through his hair.

"I don't know. I just got sick of his mouth. I guess I kind of snapped."

"Whatever it was, thanks." Ophelia smiled.

"No problem. Us bunnies have to stick together." Amry laughed.

"Well so much for our anonymous tailing of Mr. Happy. Anything we do now to watch him will be wasted. He's on alert."

"Yeah. I don't think Zachary is gonna care. He'll be who he is either way, he can't help it," Amry remarked.

"Still, something is wrong with him," Ophelia said.

"Oh, do you think?" Bethany and Sam chimed together.

"Not like he's a bad seed, more like he's hiding something. And whatever it is, it's got him all twisted up inside." Ophelia frowned.

"Lia. Really?" Amry huffed.

"Let's just forget it. He knows we're watching; we know he knows. We'll all just play the Headmasters game. Maybe Zachary will slip up, maybe he won't. I need to find out who this boy is from my vision, why Haven is calling out for Alex, and a million other things that are more important than Zachary Kowal." Ophelia frowned.

The bell interrupted with its usual clang, and the four

shuffled off. Sam and Bethany went to their next class, while Ophelia and Amry headed to their dorm room. Levitating past the tallest pine, the girls whisked through the clouds, twirling against the pale blue canvas. Flying was a freedom that one could only know in death. No constraints of a plane, jet pack, or glider, strapping you in. Just you and the vast space of unending sky.

Ophelia inhaled a deep breath, holding for a moment and then exhaling her anxiety. Floating, she soaked in the silence, allowing the calm to wash over every inch of the pure energy her celestial body contained.

Turning to Amry, her friend seemed to be enjoying their detachment from the Academy below as much as she was. A sweet smile caressed her serene face. She lay out on a blanket of air, arms stretched out to her sides, hovering in the glitter of a partially clouded sun.

"Lia. I've been thinking about your encounter with that boy," Amry spoke softly.

"And?"

"What if he's Alex?" Amry turned to Ophelia.

"Maybe. I wish I knew how to reach him. Ms. Dunworthy said to wait. She thinks it'll happen again," Ophelia sighed.

"I think so too."

"Amry, can I ask you something? But promise you won't get mad." Ophelia sat up.

"Sure." Amry rolled to her side.

"The way you were with Zachary in the cafeteria, you think it could be anger that you are still feeling toward Jeffrey?"

Amry lay there looking past Ophelia before answering.

"He hurt me more than I want to admit, so yes, you could be right. I know you think I dated a lot when I was still a breather, but the truth is, I didn't. In fact, I only had one boyfriend and he was it for me. We spent all our free time together, making plans for the future. I wanted to go to UCLA. John was going to apply there too, so we could be together." Amry's eyes grew more doleful with each word.

"His name was, John?"

"Yup. John SanSeverino. I would have been Mrs. Amry SanSeverino one day. But I guess the stars had other plans."

Ophelia's chest ached. Amry's green eyes were always bright, welcoming. Not today. The more she spoke of John, the darker they grew. She had no idea the hidden pain her friend kept to herself.

"How come you never told me about him?" Ophelia's eyes widened.

"If you think losing Jeffrey was upsetting, it was nothing compared to letting go of John. I was ripped from him by the evil demon called fate. We had our entire lives to live, saying good-bye to him was the hardest thing I've ever done. And now I wonder, who's taking my place? Is he married? Does he have kids? Christ, it's been nearly forty years. He's what, fifty-seven now. He might even have grandchildren. Or worse, what if he died already. I don't know that either. He never came here, so if he did, he was complete. And what does that mean for us. He no longer missed me? Loved me?" Amry let go and fell to the ground, stopping inches before the grass and landing on her feet.

Ophelia followed.

"I'm sorry. I didn't mean to upset you."

"It's okay, Lia. I should have told you about him a long time ago. It's just easier not to think about it."

"I understand. There are days when I am really happy and then, Haven's memory creeps in and I fall into a depression. You keep them tucked away deep in your heart." Ophelia stroked Amry's soft brown locks.

Amry reached out and hugged her best friend.

"It's different for you. We're gonna find Haven, and when

we do, you can both take the light and join your parents." Amry let go.

"Come on, let's go to our room. We have about thirty minutes to the next class and there's something I want to show you." Amry's eyes twinkled.

The girls shut the door to their door room and settled on their beds. Amry closed her eyes and extended her hand toward a blank wall next to Ophelia's side of the room.

"Watch." Amry stiffened her back.

Colors appeared, frolicking across the blank canvas, and taking shape. Ophelia's jaw dropped as she watched the pictures of Amry's life unfold in front of her. Amry as a baby, then around ten or eleven, and finally, a sixteen-year-old girl. A boy stood beside her, his arms around her shoulders as he nuzzled her cheek.

"How are you doing this?" Ophelia stuttered.

"You're not the only one with tricks, Lia."

"Is that John?"

Amry opened her eyes. If tears could form, they'd be streaming down her cheeks. But no longer among the breathing, her eyes held all the emotion through their color. And hers were the darkest green Ophelia had ever seen them.

"Yes. This is right before I got sick. We were going to a concert; the band was Jethro Tull. He surprised me for my birthday. It was both the best, and one of the worst nights of my life."

"How come?" Ophelia sat watching Amry's movie playing out on her wall.

"Because it was night, I first knew something was wrong. The concert was great, we had a blast. After it was over, we decided to go grab a burger. We were both starving. We ordered our food, and I had to use the bathroom. I had about three large sodas at the concert, and there was no waiting. I remember going to the restroom, washing my hands and then nothing. Next thing I know, I'm waking up in an ambulance. John was by my side. He told me I had passed out on my way back to the booth. They couldn't wake me up and someone called for help." Amry studied the reel of her life.

"Here, you see. We're at the hospital. That's my mom and dad. My two sisters had to wait in the lobby with my grandmother. They were too young to come up to the room. Now wait for it—my mom goes into hysterics after they told us the news. Apparently, a blood test revealed the cancer. This is the part where they explained about an oncologist, MRI's and all the junk I was about to do. John was a rock. He was so sure I'd beat it. He never wavered. Not even at the end, he always had hope."

"Oh god, Amry. I had no idea you had to deal with all this." Ophelia wiped her eyes. The tears were not there, but the pain was.

"Lia, it's no different than any other kid here. We all had lives; we were all ripped away from the people we loved before we even got a chance to really live. My story is no more heart breaking than yours."

"What is this?" Ophelia leaned forward.

"Oh. That's Amsterdam, Thailand, and Italy. My parents were determined to pack the world into whatever time I had. So, before I got really sick and could no longer travel, they took me everywhere they could. And they paid for John, too. The treatment wasn't working, so I made the choice. No more wasted days of nausea and body pain. If I could have a few good months with everyone, then I was gonna take it. And they made sure it was the best time of my life. It couldn't replace living a life with the guy I loved, but they tried." Amry's lip quivered. "Look, this is my last moment with John."

Ophelia fought to hold back the heaviness in her chest. Straining to swallow, she pushed to get past the knot in her throat before gasping. Lying at death's door, her best friend's eyes fluttered as she tried to keep them focused on John. Her pale, gray skin was like tissue paper covering the small skeleton of a life once filled with brilliance. He held her hand over his heart, tears streaming wildly down his cheeks and dripping from his chin, as he told her over and over how much he loved her. The words brushed across Ophelia's ears. His passion filling each syllable for his dying love.

Amry's parents were on the other side of the bed, her mother barely able to stand. Clinging to her husband's firm arm with one hand, she stroked her daughter's hair with the other.

As the last breath left Amry's body, John professed their eternal bond and that he would wait to be with her again. Her last vision was of his head nestled on her chest.

The pictures stopped.

Amry lay down on her bed and began humming. "What's that music you're humming?" Ophelia asked. "*You're My Best Friend* by Queen. John really liked it, I guess we both did. We were gonna play it at our wedding someday."

She was silent for a moment before continuing. "All these years, and I still miss him so much. I know we were too young for him to keep his promise to wait for me. He had a whole world in front of him. But maybe, this song may still play from time to time, and he thinks of me. Remembers who we were and the love we shared." Amry rolled over and got up.

"He does," Ophelia murmured.

"He does what?"

"Still thinks of you. I know it." Ophelia slowly blinked.

Amry smiled.

"We'd better go. You know my tardiness record; Sam isn't the only ass that'll be grass."

After they parted ways, Ophelia found herself in front of her English class with no memory of getting there. She couldn't focus on anything else but Amry. The love she had and lost, the life she led in a short time. She had always known her best friend was remarkable, now she knew to what extent. All these years of helping Ophelia, Amry never once revealed her own sadness. She quietly held her pain inside. If, no, when, she finds Haven, they can't take the light until Amry is ready. No matter how long it takes, they're not leaving her behind.

OPHELIA MEET ALEX

Ophelia's newfound mystery weighed heavy on her hope. *If this guy were Alex, how could he help her and Haven? Why him? And how were they going to do it? He's in the living dimension, or so it seemed. And why was she the only one who could see him? The rest of the class thought she had gone more insane than usual.* The questions fired like bullets, shredding her brain, if she had a brain.

The hours turned into days and the absence of new sightings began to take their toll. Ophelia retreated into the darkness. Skipping classes and spending more and more time in her room. Until the dream.

OPENING the window to the courtyard below, she scanned the students for a familiar face. Amry was sitting at a picnic table reading her favorite book, a time travel romance, *Unthreaded*. Ophelia recognized it from the cover. Hoping to catch her friend before first period, Ophelia quickly showered, dressed, and made it there just as Amry was getting up.

"Hey, I wondered when you were gonna wake up." Amry placed a bookmark on the page and closed it.

"Yeah. I know." Ophelia groaned, "I wish I knew why I still do this. Don't you guys ever get tired?"

"Nope. We're dead. How are we possibly gonna get tired? I think it's a psychological thing." Amry curled her lip.

Amry's father was a child psychologist, and often practiced what he preached. His doting daughter, a sponge for anything her dad said, was intuitive.

"Really? You're gonna pull the psych card on me?" Ophelia frowned.

"Psych card? Wow. You're starting to sound like a real twentieth century girl." Amry grinned.

"I am a real twentieth century girl."

"Barely. I don't think the ten years you spent in the beginning of the century had much influence on your current choice of verbiage."

"Oh no?"

"Nope. That's all me." Amry lightly punched Ophelia in the shoulder. "On a more serious note, you've been really scaring me lately. I thought you had plummeted back down to that dreaded place you were in when I first got here. I was planning an intervention. The gang was ready. We had spells and everything." Amry grinned. "But here you are. This makes me happy and yet question, what's changed?" Amry pressed her forehead to Ophelia's.

"I had another dream with Haven, or vision, whatever it is. I was able to hear her clearly; she was definitely shouting out the name Alex—Alex McKenna. There was a picture of The Academy of Souls on the wall, and she kept pointing to it. And then another picture of a school that resembled the Academy, but different." Ophelia pulled back.

"Different how?" Amry's eyes widened.

"Like modern. Maybe more your time. It was and it wasn't

our school. It made no sense, but she kept pointing over and over, so I think it's a major clue. When I woke up, the darkness was gone. I felt stronger."

"Maybe it's time to take this to Headmaster Abernathy. He might be able to help us."

"Not yet. I'd like to give it a few more days. I want to know, I do. But I have this feeling I'm going to see Alex very soon."

"Oh, we're calling him Alex, now?" Amry furrowed her brow.

"I think it's him, and I'm going with that for now." Ophelia gazed at the other students.

"Okay, Lia. We'll wait. I gotta head out. Calculus is about to start, and I can't be late. One more tardy and it's straight to detention. Who would have ever thought being dead still meant being on time?

"I think the Headmaster is just trying to give us a feeling of normalcy. You know, by maintaining the routine."

"Hmmm, maybe you're right. But it's still a drag."

"Well, I need to go too. I promised our resident bully I'd meet him at the library to help with the math homework." Ophelia rolled her eyes.

"Hmm. Getting pretty chummy with the bad boy?" Amry goaded her.

"What? No way. We're supposed to watch him. That's what I'm doing," Ophelia huffed.

"Those who protest too loudly ..." Amry teased.

"Cut it out. Go already, you're gonna be late." Ophelia nudged her friend.

As Amry floated down the courtyard, Ophelia tried to imagine what it would be like to take the light. Not knowing if she'd ever see her friends again tugged at her heart. But reuniting with Haven, and her parents, was everything.

The library was on the other side of the campus and

gliding would get her there in a snap, but the day glowed with droplets of sunshine on the dew of the new grass, and Ophelia preferred to walk in the beauty. She drenched in the colors of the landscape and smiled, death's little pleasures.

Zachary was already there when she arrived. He sat with his book in his lap, feet up on the table and eyes closed.

Great, she thought. *This is gonna be fun—not.*

"My dear Ophelia, I see you have no comprehension of time."

"How did you know it was me? Your eyes are closed."

"Your scent." Zachary plopped his feet down and sat up.

"What scent? You can smell me?"

"You are the only one here that has one. And yes, I can smell you. But so can everyone else."

Ophelia was dumbfounded. None of her friends ever mentioned it to her.

"I thought none of you could smell any longer?" Ophelia scanned the room.

"We cannot. A side effect I am not happy with. I miss the lovely aroma of roasting pork as the fat drips off the side, sizzling to the ground. It is only you that tickles our nose."

Ophelia inched closer and sat. She would talk to her friends later.

"Never mind," she said authoritatively. Zachary sat back and closed his eyes again.

"If you're not going to look at the book, how are you gonna learn anything?" Ophelia snapped.

"I thought you would read, and I shall learn," Zachary replied with a snarky tone.

"Forget it. I'm not here to do it for you, participate or I leave."

Pushing up in his chair, he dropped the book on the table and opened it.

Ophelia pursed her lips.

"What has you bothered now?" he asked.

"Nothing. Learn."

When they had gone through all the equations in the chapter, and Zachary had a glimmer of a handle on the answers, Ophelia announced they were finished. She had been exhausted from the dream of Haven, and now working with Zachary just drained her even more.

She figured he didn't mind, because he closed the book immediately and sliced through the heavy oak door within seconds.

Fanning the pages of the calculus book, she whiffed in the scent of paper and ink one more time. Unaware of the curious glances from the students around her, Ophelia halfheartedly headed for the exit.

First period was science. Luckily, it was only two doors away from the library, and Ophelia's favorite class. After sitting down, she searched for her friends. Bethany and Sam never sat in the same seat. Playing musical chairs seem to tickle them more than the teacher, Mrs. Santucci. Mrs. S., for short, kept her shoulder length, red locks neatly pulled back in a low bun. Her striking dark eyes were a contrast to her cupid round face. Standing at only five feet two inches, she still managed to tower over anyone who challenged her authority. She had been a teacher in life, so it was a natural transition for her at the Academy. And, although patience was a virtue she mastered, Ophelia's friends tested her relentlessly. Today, Sam was at the back of the class by one of the three large windows cut out of the west wall.

"Hey, why don't you come up here by me?" Ophelia waved to her friend. "There's two seats open."

"Nah. You come back here. I like it by the window, saved you a seat." Sam pointed to the open chair.

Ophelia was at odds. She wanted to sit by her friends, but she also didn't want to upset Mrs. S. by changing seats.

"Ophelia, come on."

"Ahem. Go on Miss Wetherton," A voice urged from the front of the class.

Ophelia whipped her head around and Mrs. S. was seated at her desk. The teacher gestured with a nod of her chin, and a smile, that it was okay for Ophelia to move. Mouthing the words *thank you,* Ophelia quietly gathered her things. With her eyes on the floor, she glided to the back of the room. She hated drawing attention to herself, especially from a teacher.

"I dread the way you tease her every day. Mrs. S. is so sweet, can't you just sit in your assigned seats?" Ophelia furrowed her brow.

"What fun is that?" Sam smirked.

"Speaking of two, where is Bethany?" Ophelia glanced at the empty seat.

"I was about to ask if you had seen her. She didn't meet me this morning. It's not like her." Sam raised a brow.

"That is odd."

Ophelia gazed out the floor to ceiling window to the outside world. The sky was a deep blue. Charcoal clouds quickly filled the crevices usually reserved for hues of orange and gold. The atmosphere had changed since this morning. She shivered.

"Knock that off," Sam ordered.

"What did I do?" Ophelia widened her eyes.

"The shivering. It's ridiculous. I swear girl, there's something seriously wrong with you."

"I don't know why it bothers you so much. I thought you said you were past all that.

"I did. But damn, it's still strange. You're not a breather but not a total spirit, what are you? I think I only want answers." He poked her arm with his pen.

"Ouch!" Ophelia rubbed her arm.

"See. Right there, that's what I'm talking about. How the in the hell did you feel that?"

Ophelia turned her head away from him. Life was life, and death was ... well, death was eternal. This shouldn't be happening and yet, here she was engaged in another pointless conversation about the oddities that were Ophelia Wetherton.

"I'm sorry, Ophelia. You know my mouth and brain don't always work well together. I can be a real air head." Sam reached for her hand, but she retracted.

Ophelia looked up at the ceiling and swiveled around with her back to Sam. She shook her head in agreement. It was the only way she could answer him without revealing how he had pierced her heart. She should be used to Sam's juvenile sense of humor by now. But some days it wore her down.

She tried to block out the painful sadness that gripped her. Mrs. S.'s words faded, leaving a resounding blah, blah, blah. Once again, her mind drifted to her chance meeting with the mystery boy she had resolved to call Alex. Tracing the moment in her mind, she struggled to look for any clue that would help her reach him again. Preoccupied, she hadn't noticed the breeze humming within the confines of the classroom. It was the chatter of female voices that broke her thought and finally got her attention.

Turning to shush the perpetrators, she was surprised when she found the rest of the class with their noses down, reading. Giggling behind her caused her body to pivot around toward the back of the class—nothing. The breeze whisked by catching the back of her hair and swishing it around her shoulders. Ophelia stood.

"Miss Wetherton, is everything all right?" Mrs. S. questioned.

Ophelia furiously scanned the classroom, nothing.

"Yes. It's just, did you feel that breeze?" Ophelia said timidly.

"No, not at all. Please, return to your seat."

Ophelia sat, her face burning. She opened her science book to the assigned page and lowered her head, leaving enough space to be able to see around the classroom. When she peered to her right, the frenetic pounding of her phantom heart seized her chest. Ophelia took a closed fist and punched her breastbone to gain control of the beating. A gaping hole not more than four feet in front of her, with its edges peeled back, revealed a line of lockers with three teenage girls laughing at a boy in a Letterman's jacket. Their clothes suggest modern society, like what Alex wore.

Slowly reaching out, she cautiously put her hand up to the window into the other world. A cool stream of air moved in a circular motion around the inside of the passage. Gently, she pushed her right hand through. A shrill scream startled her, and she snapped back. The three girls were staring directly at her, remarking to the boy about a hand from nowhere appearing in the hall. Ophelia shot up, but they didn't react. She made a waving gesture, but they didn't seem to see her. *They only saw my hand when it punctured the divide between us. They can't see me, or us.*

Ophelia stood enamored in front of the open gateway. A bell rang, theirs. The hall was quickly taken over by scores of yammering students. *There's so many of them.* She thought.

Studying their interaction, she grinned. The kids of today were so different than the classmates she'd had in her time. They never would have been so boisterous and loud. That was grounds for detention. And she nearly fell over when two of the students, both boys, were making out in front of one of the lockers. Her gasp must have been loud because it caught the attention of Leon Brickman. Best friend to Roger Mooring and Ophelia's unwanted science partner.

"Sit down mouse, you dumb ass weirdo." Leon moved her chair out.

Ophelia hated him as much as she did, Roger. They were friends when they were breathers, thieves actually. But not the grab and run type of hooligan. Roger and Leon were much worse. They would break into rich folks' homes, mostly the lavish Victorian style. Those were the ones with the bucks. If the poor residents happen to be home, they would tie them up and beat them. They said it was to keep them from telling the police. One family did though, the boys made the mistake of stealing the owner's prize thoroughbred. They were tracked down, found guilty in a trial that lasted forty-five minutes, and hung in the center of town two days before Christmas, December 23, 1865. The Headmaster was baffled when they arrived, or so the story goes. He knew eventually *The Nowhere* would take them, until then however, they were the burden of the Academy.

Ophelia was relieved when Leon was finally forced into *The Nowhere* by a visiting, extremely skilled, young sorcerer. It was two calm years. Roger didn't act up as much once he was on his own. Everyone was flabbergasted when he returned. He had done the nearly impossible and escaped the clutches of darkness.

"Shut up, Leon. Stop calling me, mouse. What does that even mean?" Ophelia whispered.

"You're like a little gray mouse that I could squash with my shoe. That's what it means." Leon gritted his teeth.

Ophelia wouldn't be intimidated by him, not today. Concentrating on the sea of students, she desperately scoured for the one teen she was focused on—Alex. Coming around the corner from another hallway, he was headed right toward her. Holding hands with a cute brunette, they were exchanging dialogue, eyes locked. She inched closer to the opening. The thought of it closing before she had a chance to communicate burrowed into her mind. Anxiety churned the pit of her stomach, forcing a volcanic mock acid to rise to the back of her throat. She couldn't wait any longer, without realizing the volume, the words passed through her lips puncturing the gateway and capturing the attention of Alex McKenna.

Alex stalled in place, turning from Margaret, his gaze migrated to Ophelia.

"What the heck are you looking at?" Margaret asked.

"It's her. The girl I told you about. The one I saw earlier." Alex stared.

'Haven?" Margaret circled around.

"No. The teenage girl."

"Alex, I don't see anything." Margaret frowned.

"I don't think anyone does. Just me."

Ophelia's body shook, *he is Alex.* She moved closer.

"Who are you?" Alex questioned.

The cool air embraced his surroundings, and a shiver danced along his spine.

Ophelia blinked, her mouth hanging open. He was right in front of her, and nothing came out.

"Do you need help? Are you friends with ... Haven?" Alex questioned.

Ophelia gulped. He did know her.

"Ophelia. My name is Ophelia. Haven is my ..."

A sudden twist of wind kicked up and knocked her back. She lost her balance and fell to the floor. She cried out in horror as the portal swirled violently and then snapped shut. The last thing she saw was Alex, reaching out for her.

WHERE'S BETHANY?

lex remained long after the last bell rang for class. Margaret had slid down against the wall, waiting for some signs of life.

"Hello? Are you in there?" Margaret joked.

"Yeah. I'm here. But I think something is pulling me there."

"Where?"

"To Ophelia," he murmured.

"Wait. What?" Margaret hastily rose to her feet. "Where is it you think you're going?"

"I'm not really sure." Alex raised a brow.

"That's it. We're calling your Gram."

Alex's great grandmother often assisted him in the difficult cases.

"We don't need to bother my Gram. I know what I need to do. The next time this doorway opens, I'm walking through it."

"Are you kidding me with this shit? You don't know who that girl is, where that place is, and for all you know it's some kind of cosmic trap," Margaret argued.

"I don't think it's a trap. She's connected to Haven somehow.

I think they both need my help," Alex argued.

"Do you remember what happened with the last case? You almost died because of your thick skull." Margaret blinked to fight back the tears.

Alex relaxed his shoulders. Wrapping his arms around her waist, he pulled her close. Sometimes he could get so wrapped up in the spirits that needed him, he forgot about the people close to him. Margaret was frightened for him; he should have known that.

"I promise *ciuccia mia*, no rash decisions this time. When she comes again, I'll be ready."

"Ready how?" Margaret wiped a tear from her cheek.

"I'll cast a protection spell as soon as the gateway opens." Alex kissed her salty lips.

Margaret nuzzled her head into his chest.

"You can't die."

"I won't."

SILENCE FILLED the crevices of the McKenna household, and for the first time since Alex could remember, it replaced his peace with an ominous void.

He texted Margaret to see what time she'd be over. Her worry for him had gone into overdrive this afternoon. Which boggled him a little, considering the nature of their last case. In his mind, five ghastly deaths and a giant demon from hell trumped a teenage girl from a ghostly dimension. Whatever it was that hooked Margaret's fear radar, he would talk to her tonight when she got there. This was supposed to be their time. The house was theirs, the big case solved, and Christmas vacation was around the corner. The ideal setting for an Alex & Margaret, munch, cuddle, and binge-watching weekend.

He tried to shake off the melancholy, but it didn't want to retreat. He thought it might be the residue left behind by Ophelia, the teen he encountered earlier. Picturing her, the name fit her. He knew by the appearance of her wavering body she was a spirit, so were the other kids in her class. *How odd*. He thought. The idea that there was a class comprised only of celestial beings lit a flame of curiosity. This was a new one for him. He had seen many things growing up. From demons to angels, to trapped souls, but this one really intrigued him.

Ambling into the kitchen, he assessed the snack situation before deciding on Funny Bones and orange juice. Balancing the plate, the glass, and some chips—just in case the chocolaty goodness wasn't enough—he retreated to his bedroom on the second floor.

Pulling out some of his family's journals, Alex flipped through the pages searching for anything that could explain his encounter. Luckily, he had the luxury of having the books in his possession. It was only recently that his mom opened and accepted the family gift of paranormal sensitivity. She had struggled to deny it for years, thinking it would keep Alex and his little brother Wilby, safe. Eventually, it became evident that it only put them at risk. After the Geranium deaths, she brought the books out from hiding. Alex soaked up the words like a sponge. Wilby, being only ten, was more interested in his video games.

Halfway through the third chapter in a book of his family lineage, there was a brief mention about a school designed for all the wayward souls of teens who didn't cross over into the light; *The Academy of Souls*. He muttered the words aloud. It mentioned the founder, Barnabas Abernathy, and nothing more.

Alex scoured the rest of the pages searching for anything

that would give him additional information, but there was nothing beyond the short paragraph. Pulling his phone from his pocket, he called his grandmother.

She picked up after one ring.

"Alex, is everything all right?" His gram questioned.

"Hi Gram, all's good. Question. Have you heard of a high school for spirits called The Academy of Souls?" Alex placed his phone on speaker mode and set it on the bed.

"Sure. It was started by Barnabas Abernathy. He's Headmaster for the school. Nice man, a little stuffy, but he cares deeply for all his students."

"You know him? How is it you never mentioned this before?" Alex took a sip of juice.

"It was a long time ago. A bit of a tortured soul. He had trouble with his sister and nephew if I remember correctly. Why are you asking me this, Bonzetta?"

"I think I got a glimpse of the Academy today."

"Does this have anything to do with the little girl, Haven? Is she at the school?"

"Yes and no. At least I don't think she's at the school. There's someone else, another girl. A teenager, maybe around my age. Her name is Ophelia; I think she knows Haven."

"How do you know this?" She cleared her throat.

"You have trouble swallowing again?" Alex sounded concern.

"I'm fine. Just a little cold."

"Gram, you promised you'd go to the doctor. You've had that lump in your throat for over a month," Alex pleaded.

"Never mind that. Answer my question. How do you know her name is Ophelia? Were you able to speak with her?"

"Yes, for a short time. A portal opened, twice now. At first, I thought it might just be a window, but the second time, I could feel it pulling me. I knew if I got closer, I could pass through it."

"Be very careful, a living soul doesn't belong at the Academy. I'm not sure what the consequences would be. Alex, there's a possibility you could get permanently trapped there. Don't go through, do you understand?" Gram warned.

"Okay, I gotta go. Margaret's at the door," he lied.

"Alex, tell me you'll listen,"

"I will, I will." Alex swiped the screen on his phone. Finishing the last bite of Funny Bone, he slid the books under his bed and lay down. Staring up at the ceiling, his veins pulsed with the remnants of the invisible pull to Ophelia's world. Focusing on school, his family, and his relationship with Margaret, did little to distract the magnet that pulled at his soul. His grandmother's warning crawled to the outer edges of his mind and dropped off, landing in a bottomless pit. If he needed to step into Ophelia's world of the Academy to help her and Haven, he had no choice. This is what he does, why his gifts were given to him. He wasn't about to waste them on fear. Now, to get past his biggest obstacle—Margaret.

A knock sounded from below. His gate keeper had arrived. Margaret could be a real bad ass when she wanted to, and especially protective of him. But it was a two-way street; they watched out for each other. When Alex had first stepped onto the campus of CATA, Cain Amry Thearige Academy, it wasn't easy. His psychic abilities didn't discriminate. Spirits visit wherever he is. At home, school, or pushing a cart through the grocery store. Alex had to learn how to interact without gaining attention. Not an easy thing to do. But he figured it out. His other obstacle that belonged to others, not him, was a little more difficult to navigate. The hormonal journey his body had set sail on. Causing confusion and sometimes ridicule, from a select few.

The several months it took for his doc to get his meds straight were brutal. That's when he met Margaret. Full blown battle, fighting who he knew he was, and the revolution going on within.

They had casually struck up a conversation here and there, but it wasn't until they were assigned to work as partners for a science project, that the closeness blossomed. He immediately felt drawn to her, but knowing the past, Alex kept his emotions at bay. It was Margaret who made the first move.

He had the talk with her, several months earlier. Margaret as usual, surprised him. Their relationship didn't change. Good, and not so good. She took his breath away. But he chose silence. He didn't want to scare her off. Being friends was one thing, being in a relationship came with a whole new set of instructions.

They were at his house working on the Geranium case. It was after a near death incident, and Margaret grabbed him, devouring his quivering lips. He could still remember the taste of her cherry cola lip balm.

He stopped her mid kiss. Struggling with the lump that rose in the back of his throat, he fumbled to find the words. He didn't have to. She took his hands in hers and traced the back with her thumbs. She told him none of it mattered to her. She knew how she felt. Then she asked him if he had feelings for her. Alex tried to calm the explosion that was erupting in his body. His heart pushed the walls of his chest to its limits, and he wiped his palms on the leg of his jeans. He cupped her jaw and let his fingers traced the outline of her face and settle beneath her chin. Tilting his head slightly he pressed his lips to hers, once again drinking in the cherry cola. She had been by his side ever since. Whether he chooses full surgery, or not, she is his, and he belongs to her.

Alex bolted down the stairs and opened the door to his lovely beauty. Throwing her arms around him, she held on tight. Pulling back slightly, he gazed into her soft brown eyes and the smile that melted his heart.

"Hey, you okay?" He closed the door.

"Yeah. Just ... I don't know, a feeling I've been getting today." Margaret curled her lip.

"A feeling? Sounds like you're getting some mojo of your own." Alex joked.

"I'm serious. Don't joke. I'm really worried about this case, and I don't understand why."

"Well, we're both here now. The weekend is ours and we have a lot of *us* time to catch up on. So, let's put all that aside for now, okay? I want you, the couch, some chocolate cookies, and the latest season of *Stranger Things*, binging on TV. We missed everything with our last case. I love when we get to binge on Halloween, but we can make up for it now." Alex held up a bag of generic cookies.

Margaret reluctantly nodded.

"Oh, and forget those store bought, chocolate preservative filled pieces of cardboard. I brought black and whites from Buttercooky Bakery." Margaret pulled the bag from her purse.

"Even better." Alex grabbed her waist, and they collapsed on the couch.

Lying on the plush cushions, Margaret's body entangled in his, he decided to take his own advice and not mention his plans for the next time Ophelia shows up. The nuclear reaction could wait until the weekend was over; he hoped.

OPHELIA GLIDED up and floated to her seat. Leon glared with narrowed eyes and pursed lips, shaking his head back and forth.

"There is something seriously wrong with you, mouse. Makes me wish I could cut your brain out and see what's misfiring."

Ophelia quickly turned away.

"Don't be a spaz, Leon!" Sam gently touched her forearm. "Are you okay, Ophelia?"

"I'm okay."

Ten minutes until class ended, she couldn't wait to escape the confines of Leon's damning glare. She swore that if she hadn't already been dead, he would have killed her just for fun. Evil blackened his soul, nurturing the darkness. Just like his best friend Roger, Leon had a taste for brutality.

Ophelia never looked up once in the remaining time. Keeping herself aloof to his constant annoying ways to gain recognition, it would be the only way she'd make it out of there without any further confrontation. Although Leon was a malevolent bastard, he had an extremely limited attention span. No doubt he was already plotting his new poem of verbal abuse for some unsuspecting soul in his next class.

The welcoming ring of the three o'clock bell brought a sigh of relief. Ophelia couldn't gravitate out of there fast enough. She headed straight for the courtyard where she knew Amry would be. It was their unofficial meeting spot when they both had a free period.

"Hey, Ophelia! Wait." Sam called out.

"I'm going to the courtyard. Meet me there." Ophelia didn't slow down.

Amry was lying on the grass under a large oak tree, eyes closed.

"What are you doing?" Ophelia held her hand to the sun.

"Seeing what it would be like." Amry raised her chin.

"What are talking about?" Ophelia crossed her legs and levitated down next to Amry.

"I was closing my eyes and trying to block out the sound to remember what it was like to sleep." Amry turned to Ophelia with one open eye.

"Why would you do such a thing?" Ophelia's widened her eyes.

"I don't know. I guess I wanted to feel more human. But it's not working, so let's forget about it."

"But ..." Ophelia paused.

"Really, it's okay. I was thinking about our conversation earlier, and John, that's all. It was stupid. How was Science?"

"Boring." Sam took a seat between the girls.

"What happened?" Amry sat up.

"Leon Brickman. Oh, and Ophelia had another episode." Sam studied the crowd of students drifting by. "Amry have you seen, Bethany?"

"No. Wait. Lia, what episode?" Amry tugged Ophelia's sleeve.

"That's weird." Sam stood.

"I will tell you later." Ophelia grinned at Amry.

"What's weird?" Amry looked up at Sam.

"I haven't seen Bethany since last night." He ran his hand through his hair and stopped. "I'm gonna go look for her."

"We'll help you." The girls shot up toward the clouds with the precision of skilled pilots.

Hovering above the Academy, they scoured the area for Bethany while Sam decided to check the dorm. There was no sign of her, so they floated to the cafeteria, it was empty. The library and science lab turned up nothing as well.

"Now I'm starting to get worried." Ophelia twirled to look behind her.

"Don't worry, Lia. She's probably in the bleachers, watching the new arrivals. Bethany loves to check out the new souls, you know that." Amry smiled.

"I don't know. I have this weird uttering in my belly. I think something is wrong."

Amry sighed, "Let's go check the dorm, maybe Sam found her."

They bumped into Sam on the way over, he hadn't found her.

"I don't get it. Where is she?" Sam rolled his eyes.

"When was the last time you saw her?" Amry questioned.

"I told you, last night."

"Yes, but where were you?"

"At the library. She had that English paper due tomorrow and she needed to get some information out of one of the classic books."

"Which one?" Amry narrowed her eyes.

"Oh man, what does that have to do with anything?" Sam snapped.

"Because we can go to the library and see if the book is there. If it isn't, we can see what time she checked it out and go from there. Maybe trace her steps."

"Good idea." Sam slapped Amry on the back.

"Yeah, I get them from time to time." Amry smirked.

"Wait, what do we do if the book is there?" Ophelia pushed her hair back.

"Then we're screwed, and we'll have to go to the Headmaster." Sam shook his head.

"One thing at a time. Let's see if the book is there." Amry swished up toward the roof of the dorms and darted toward the library.

Not bothering with formalities, the three teens passed through the large oak door.

"Which one was it, Sam?" Ophelia chimed.

"Of Mice and Men."

Tracing their imprints on the books as they glided down each row, they stopped when they came to the resting place of John Steinbeck's masterpiece. Ophelia stood behind Amry, who was thoroughly checking the shelves above and below where the book should be.

"It's not here. Let's go to the information desk and check the log."

In the Academy of Souls, students were left on their honor

to check out a book and then return it in a timely manner. Occasionally, someone did forget to bring one back. The librarian created the ledger for logging the time and date a book was removed.

"According to this, Bethany checked the book out at ten fifty-five last night." Amry pointed to the entry.

"That's only about fifteen minutes after I left her," Sam stammered.

"This is interesting." Amry pointed to a name on the page.

"What's that?" Sam rolled his eyes.

"There's a time stamped just a minute before Bethany's for The Catcher in the Rye."

"And? What's so odd about that?" Sam huffed.

"It was checked out by Roger Mooring." Amry raised a brow.

"Oh no," murmured Ophelia.

"What do you mean? How does any of this have anything to do with Bethany?" Sam barked.

"Don't you get it? Roger Mooring doesn't read, let alone a classic. He and Leon probably haven't picked up a book in years. Something's wrong." Amry bit the inside of her cheek.

"Leon was in class but has anyone seen Roger?" They all shook their heads negatively.

"We need to find that son of bitch. If he's hurt her ..." Sam swooped out of the building.

"Sam, wait! He's not listening. Jeez, we don't even know where to start looking." Amry turned to Ophelia.

"We need to catch up with him. I think we should stay together." Ophelia levitated.

"Agreed." Amry followed.

They caught up with Sam halfway between crazed and over the edge. He was hovering above the trees in the courtyard, scouring for signs of either Roger or Leon.

"We need to think about this." Ophelia spun around before nestling on a low cloud.

"Lia's right. Let's be smart because lord knows neither one of them are. Given that they aren't masterminds and just street thugs, where would their feeble minds bring her?" Amry closed her eyes.

"What are you doing? We're not even sure Roger's got her," Sam's voice cracked.

"It sure looked like you made up your mind a few minutes ago, when you launched out of the library like a rocket. And I'm picturing the campus of the Academy. I'm trying to see where a secluded spot might be."

"What about the showers?" Ophelia interjected.

"That is a great spot, Lia. You don't even go there." Amry's eyes sparkled.

"No. I prefer the privacy of our bathroom," Ophelia quipped.

"This isn't important. Let's try the showers, I gotta do something," Sam snapped.

"Wait. Should we tell, Dictator Dick? He's head of security, maybe he can help. Or how about Mr. Coal and Mr. Rain, it couldn't hurt," Ophelia queried.

"No. No goons," Sam retorted.

The three of them cut across the tower of the main building, keeping their airborne travel at considerable height with maximum visibility. The gym was on the other side of the Academy's grounds. Cradled between the theater and the Headmaster's quarters, the showers adjacent to the gym reflected a world they left behind. Gingerly landing on the rooftop of the building, they walked to the edge and peered down. The two large steel doors that hung in the entryway of the gym were closed.

"That's definitely odd," Ophelia stated.

"What's that?" Sam asked.

"The doors. They're always open. You know the privacy rule the Headmaster has. No walking through doors just because we can. Well, he leaves the gym open. It doesn't belong to anyone person like a dorm room, but it keeps kids from forgetting the rules and passing through. If they do it enough, they'll forget and apply it everywhere. So open door policy for the gym." Ophelia smiled.

"I guess that makes sense. I never noticed them before. Probably because I never come here. What about the library? That's a public space and the doors are always shut?" Sam furrowed his brow.

"It's a quiet place. Opening the door reminds you of that." Ophelia crossed her arms.

"Wow. You're like a brochure for The Academy of Souls.

Anything else you'd like to add?" Sam said sarcastically.

"Yup."

"What's that?"

"The doors just opened, and Leon left." Ophelia smirked. "Crap. Let's go."

They floated down the east side of the building and instead of obeying etiquette, transported through the front doors, opting to leave them shut so it wouldn't attract any unwanted attention. They had no idea what they were walking into, and at least if they could hold on to the element of surprise, they might gain the upper hand.

The electric blue bleachers with layers of undisturbed dust had not seen a team since the beginning of the Academy. Mostly jocks with unresolved hero issues came in from time to time, to relive their moments of glory. A concept that Ophelia found to be ridiculous. The room was dark, lit only by the natural stream of light reaching through the ten square windows. Five on each side, close to the ceiling. Each one no more than a foot long by a foot wide.

Drifting toward the back of the building, they passed

through a graveyard of empty lockers. Only Ophelia could appreciate the curtain of damp air brushing across her face as they floated to their destination. The walls, comprised of large gray stones, added to the eerie shivers running along the back of her celestial spine. She hovered for a moment, taking a whiff of the mildew laced cracks in the stone. A memory of the garden wall her dad had built, when they first moved into their Victorian dream house, tightened its grip in the center of her chest.

Her thoughts were interrupted by a faint pounding traveled through the hollow of the walls, resting in Ophelia's inner ear, beating along the stem of the back of her neck. She winced. The tips of her ears stung with heat the closer they floated to showers.

"Something's really wrong." Ophelia stopped and touched the ground with her feet.

"What is it, Lia?" Amry settled beside her.

"I'm getting a weird feeling. My ears are hot." She reached up and massaged the tips.

Amry leaned in to get a better look. "They're glowing red. Sam, let's walk."

"Why?" He hovered above them.

"Because. I don't know why, but it seems like we should." Amry reached up and pulled on his arm.

"Okay. I'm coming. The two of you are killing me. Oh wait— too late. Seriously though, how does it help Bethany if we enter on foot?"

"We won't create any wind, so we can be stealthier." Amry narrowed her eyes. "Good?"

"Gooood." Sam slid down between the girls.

The closer Ophelia got, the worse the burning engulfed her ears. It spread to the top of head, and down the sides of her throat. Beads of sweat drizzled down from her forehead, stinging her eyes.

"What is wrong with me?" Ophelia wiped her face with her sleeve.

"Lia, is that—sweat?" Amry leaned in.

"Damn. It is." Sam stepped back a couple of feet.

"What, you afraid it's contagious, Sam?" Ophelia hissed.

"No, sorry. It just surprised me." Sam looked down at his feet.

"It's that god-awful pounding. It's doing something to me." "What pounding?" Both Sam and Amry asked at the same time.

"You don't hear it?"

They both shook their heads in disagreement.

"The closer we get, the louder it gets and the worse I feel." Ophelia held her head.

"Well, we're here. So, let's go in and figure out what this is." Amry rubbed Ophelia's arm.

The door to the showers had a small round window, about eye level. Ophelia pressed her forehead to the glass and swiveled her head.

"I don't see anything." She closed her eyes and heaved in a heavy breath. "Let's go in." She pushed through the door.

She took one step through the doorway, and Ophelia collapsed to the ground.

"It's so loud," she shouted.

"Lia, can you figure out where it's coming from?"

Ophelia struggled to focus as the sound shredded her ears. Folding her knees to her chest, she wrapped her arms around her legs. Rocking back and forth, she was unable to pinpoint the origin of the painful noise.

"We gotta do something, this is torturing her," Amry pleaded with Sam.

"You check the right set of showers; I'll check the left." Sam pointed.

Amry nodded and sped to the right. At the end of the last stall, was a small door no more than four feet tall.

"Sam, come here."

He was beside her in a blink.

"Check this out. It's a little door. Can you go get Lia and bring her here? Let's see if this is where it's coming from."

Sam carried Ophelia in his arms and set her down next to the door. She screamed.

"That's it, I'm going in." Amry gripped the knob.

"No. I have to go. I'm the only one who hears it." Ophelia placed her hand over Amry's.

"We'll both go." Amry opened the door.

"We'll all go." Sam wrapped his arms around Ophelia and slid her through, "What is this?" Sam stood.

"It looks like a tunnel. A very dark, creepy tunnel." Amry backed up to Sam.

"It stopped. When you pulled me through, the banging went away." Ophelia struggled to stand.

"Here, let me help you." Sam lifted her from under her arm.

"I guess we're in the right place. But the question is, where?"

Amry intertwined her fingers with Ophelia's.

"Yeah. And who wants us here?" Ophelia whispered.

"And where the hell is Bethany?" Sam demanded.

"Let's follow this tunnel and see where it leads. I don't think we have a choice." Amry squeezed Ophelia's hand. "You okay?"

"Yes. I'm fine."

The ground beneath their feet chipped away with centuries of neglect. Water trickled from the cracks in the stacked stones, cascading its way down to the bottom surface. A thin layer polished the path, making it slick to the touch.

To move about quietly, the three friends hovered a couple

of inches above the surface. Gliding felt good to Ophelia, who minutes ago was in a sound stage for hell. The cool, damp air gently whispered to her, as she allowed the breeze to sooth the remnants of stinging mock flesh.

The deeper they went, the less light they had. At least a mile away from any windows to aid them, the blackness that crept over the walls of the tunnel draped a veil of darkness over their vision. Ophelia put her hand up to her face, nothing. Complete blindness had taken over.

"Hold hands and don't let go. Sam grabbed one of us." Amry reached out.

"I'm here," Sam confirmed.

"I have him," Ophelia replied.

"Move very slow. This is wickedly treacherous. I can't tell where the walls are."

"Spread out. This tunnel isn't that wide. We should be able to touch either side of the walls, and stay together," Sam stated.

Sam held a rm grip on Ophelia and reached out with his free hand. His fingertips brushed along the uneven stones.

"I've got my side. What about you, Amry?" Sam asked.

"Me too," replied Amry.

"Great. Now don't let go and keep moving forward."

"Poor Lia. You're like a rag doll being pulled apart."

"I will be all right as long as neither one of you decides to speed up without the other," Ophelia whispered.

"Why are you whispering?" Amry questioned.

"I'm not sure. I feel like I have to."

"Hey. You girls see that?"

"No. What?" The girls replied.

"A flash of light. I swear—there. See it?"

Sam exclaimed. "I did."

"Me too." Ophelia widened her eyes.

Slowly inching toward the scintillating gleam of ghoulish

green light, Ophelia gulped. They abruptly froze when the low rumble of voices echoed through the passage. "Did you hear that?" whispered Sam.

"Yeah. It sounds like more than one voice." Amry turned her head sideways.

"Wait. What is that?" Ophelia let go of her friends.

"It's sounds like a whistle." Amry crept a few inches.

"That's not a whistle, it's wind howling." Ophelia reached out for Amry.

"Why would wind be howling like that down here?" Sam scoffed.

"A portal," Ophelia mumbled.

"Jeez. Like the one in science class?" Sam's voice rose.

"Shh. Right now, whoever that is, they don't know we're here. Let's keep it that way." Amry squinted to see Sam's silhouette. She gripped his arm.

The glow intensified, illuminating the tunnel in front of them.

"At least we can see now," Ophelia muffled her voice.

"Yeah. But is that a good thing or a bad thing? Do we *want* to see what's down there?" Amry questioned.

"Sarcasm?" Ophelia clutched the back of her friends' blouse.

"Sarcasm," Amry retorted.

In a line like lambs to slaughter, they followed the ominous green, yellow glow. The closer they got, the louder and more pronounced the voices became. Roger Moorings sharp tone snapped like a whip, peeling back the layers of Ophelia's would be flesh with every strike. The agonizing pleas belonged to Bethany.

Ophelia gasped just as Sam recognized the voice of his love. Flaring nostrils, tight jaw, and a rigid cold glare, masked over his usual boyish good looks. Anticipating his next move, she pierced through his celestial wave and stood in front of him.

"Stop. You cannot go charging in there. We don't know what kind of danger Bethany's in. If you recklessly barrel in without a plan, then we could cause more harm." Ophelia stood straight, fists clenched.

"We don't know what he's doing to her!" Sam took a step. "That's exactly Lia's point. We need to be smart about this."

Amry clenched his hand.

"Listen, Sam. We both know you want to send Roger to Hades and you're worried about Bethany. We are too. So, let's do this the right way and get her back safe." Ophelia touched his forehead with hers. "We are in this together, right?"

"Right." Sam pulled back. "What's the plan?"

"I think one of us should go in first and distract him. The other two can follow shortly after, hopefully surprising Roger enough to gain control and grab Bethany. Then the four of us get out of this nasty place ..." Ophelia put her hands on her hips.

"Look at you go, Wonder Woman." Amry winked.

"Wonder ...? Never mind. I'll go first." Ophelia gravitated toward the light.

"Careful, Lia. We have no idea what that light is. Look, it's gone from glowing green to fiery red." Amry pointed.

Ophelia whipped her head back to the opening at the end of the tunnel. Amry was right. The light radiated with the intensity of one's image of the inferno in hell. Blinding her eyes, the closer she got, she moved her hand in front of her face and cocked her head to the side. A skewed view enabled her to go forward. Roger's voice was clear now and so was Bethany's.

"Please, Roger. Don't do this. You'll condemn my soul for eternity," Bethany's voice quivered.

"You should have told me yes. This would all be different," Roger bellowed.

"What would all be different?" Ophelia glided through the archway, staying close to the wall. The intense shine followed a straight path. Nothing beyond its radius was illuminated.

"Lia! Go back. He's crazy. He'll hurt you," Bethany pleaded. Roger had Bethany's hands tied at the wrist with a gold binding rope. The only restraint that works on a celestial. His left arm folded around her neck and the other held a small book.

"Lia, please. He'll push you into the vortex."

Ophelia's gaze traveled to the fiery glow of prismatic colors. It was mesmerizing. Red, yellow, green, and blue. Distracted by Bethany when she first entered the hell hole, she hadn't noticed the wind growing in the corner of the den, more ferocious than any hurricane she'd seen as a breather.

"Ophelia! It's the gateway to *The Nowhere*. He opened it!" Bethany screamed.

Jolting back, Ophelia broke the link between her gaze and the consuming aberration. Her mind scrambled for a plan to pull Roger from his obsession.

"Why are you doing this, Roger? Bethany barely knows you." Ophelia scanned the room for something helpful to use against him.

"Well that's it, isn't it? I've tried over and over again to get some kind of reaction from this bitch. But she's got her hip attached to that loser, Sam. Last night at the library, I decided to give her one more chance. One more go at it. Open her eyes to me, and to forget that piece of shit she's been wasting her time on." Roger leered.

"What did you do?"

Ophelia kept talking to him. She needed to distract him long enough for their plan to work.

"I said Roger, what in heavens did you do?" Ophelia snapped.

"'I dosed her. With the pages of the book," Roger said proudly.

Dosing is a potion made from the essence of the in-between world of Condemned Wizard Souls. It's nearly impossible to come by. One has to actually travel to the realm and make it back. A di cult task because most of the souls there have gone mad. If you're trapped, they torture the celestial by performing dark magic on them, day after day.

"How did you get it?" Ophelia heard movement behind her but didn't react.

"I have friends. Well, Leon has friends. He helped me. I sprinkled some on the pages while Leon distracted her. Her soul went into a catatonic state. He helped me get her here. I've been professing my affections all night, but the bitch is deaf."

Bethany trembled as she struggled to break free from the madman's grip. Her face scrunched, her eyes the size of saucers. Ophelia knew what she was truly frightened of, and it wasn't Roger. One thrust and he could catapult her into the in nite abyss of, *The Nowhere*. She had to keep him talking. Ophelia could feel the change of the air as Sam and Bethany skirted around the shadows of the walls, and away from the penetrating rays at the mouth of the cyclone.

"Since when do you care, Roger? It seems as long as I have been here at the Academy, you and Leon never worry about anyone else. It's always been just the two of you. Why is that Roger?"

Roger's eyes twitched.

"Are you sure it's Bethany, and not Leon you really want?" Ophelia continued to needle him.

"I mean, if that's how you really feel, why not tell everyone? No one here would care, and you could let Bethany be with whoever she wants. You both win."

Ophelia shook when Roger slammed the book on the ground and tightened his grip on Bethany's throat.

"Forgive me. I'm sorry Roger. Please ease your grip, you're hurting her."

Bethany clawed at Roger's hands, trying to peel back one finger at a time. But he was too strong. His energy was much older than hers. The longer you're dead, the more powerful you become. Channeling his connection with the universe, Roger's circuits were fueled by anger. Sparks of blue light sizzled off the tips of his fingers, dissolving and soaking in Bethany's energy, slowly draining her.

"You're sorry? I don't give a crap. We should have tossed you into *The Nowhere* a long time ago. Stupid girl. The only reason you're still here is because Leon loved torturing you. Otherwise, you'd be banished to the darkness." Roger bent his knees to reach for the book.

"Psyche." Sam emerged from the shadows with the discarded book in his hand.

"Give it to me or your bitch goes in now." Roger dangled Bethany's limp body toward the opening.

"Let her go you waste of space, or I'll toss your book in." Sam held the book up.

Keeping Roger's attention at bay was working. He never noticed Amry. She had slipped past Sam and creeping along the wall, the gray stone, and shadows, cloaked her. Hovering just behind Roger's vision, she was about to lunge when a sixth soul crashed the party.

"Why is she still here? And what's up with the crowd?" Leon hovered at the archway.

"I was getting ready to send little miss *too good* through, when I was very rudely interrupted." Roger glared at Ophelia and then Sam.

"I don't give a rats ass, throw her in already. I need to get over to the library and return that book. We don't want any unwanted attention. Where is the book?" Leon moved toward the center of the room.

"Uh, uh, uh. Stay where you are, you piece of crap." Sam waved the book in the air. "What is so important about this damn book anyway?"

"It opened the vortex." Bethany whispered.

Ophelia turned to Sam; whose mouth was clenched tighter than the lock on Headmaster Abernathy's office door.

The iron latch was forged in the pit of Lucifer's fire, the name given to the in-between realm that was prone to unending volcanic eruptions. Headmaster rescued a wrongly accused soul

that had been banished there. As a thank you, the man, who as a breather was a blacksmith, created the intricate lock as a gift.

"Put her down, Roger. And then I'll give you back your book." Sam inched closer.

"Stop right there, Burkletter. Roger, don't listen to him. Once you drop his slut, he'll throw the book in." Leon's words dripped with disdain.

"What did you call her?" Sam roared.

"Sam. Wait. Don't ..." Ophelia reached out to grab him.

But she was too late. Sam spiraled up and then dropped like a bomb on the top of Roger's shoulders, sending Bethany collapsing to the ground. Releasing his grip, Sam dropped down beside Bethany and scooped her up in his arms.

Leon charged toward them, but Ophelia managed to grab the tail end of his shirt and yank. The two of them catapulted back, slamming into the wall.

With a maddening roar, Roger took flight and swooped around the ceiling of the tunnel, drawing speed. Aiming his desire for hate, he soared straight for Sam and Bethany. "Now, you'll both go," Roger's demonic tone echoed.

"I don't think so," Amry shouted.

Before Roger realized what was happening, Amry broke free from the protection of the darkness and rammed into his unsuspecting spirit. Losing control, he tumbled in flight and fell to the ground. Seeing this, Ophelia quickly rushed to help her friend. The two girls grabbed Roger from the back of his arms and levitated. Standing directly in front of the mouth to *The Nowhere*, they swung his dazed body into the mouth of the ferocious vortex, feeding its hunger and snapping it shut.

Sam removed the bondage from Bethany's wrists and raised her up into his arms, holding her close to his chest. She murmured and then fainted.

"I got to get her out of here. Almost all her energy is drained. I'm taking her to Ms. Dunworthy."

"Wait. What's a shrink gonna do?" Amry asked.

"She's also a healer." Sam shouted as they soared down the tunnel.

"Hmm. Didn't know that." Amry glanced over at Leon. Ophelia picked up the small book from the ground. Blowing off the remnants of the tunnel floor, she opened it.

"Amry, there's a whole lot more here than just instructions on how to open the doorway to *The Nowhere*. There's also a map and guide to all the in-between realms. Listen, it says ..."

Ophelia was interrupted by gurgling groans from Leon. "How about we talk more about that in our dorm. I think we should get out of here before he wakes up and realizes his better half has been obliterated."

"Sure. Good idea." Ophelia nuzzled the book close to her chest and took fight.

"Lia, no. We don't have time for that." Amry reached out and grabbed Ophelia's hand.

"But Headmaster ..." Ophelia raised a brow.

"I'm pretty sure he'd rather us break the rules and stay our perky, celestial selves." Amry squeezed her grip.

In moments they were standing in the center of their dorm room.

"What do you think we should do with this book? I mean it is checked out to Roger." Ophelia lay on the bed flipping through the pages.

"I think we keep it. For now." Amry looked out of the window.

"What do you see?" Ophelia sat up.

"Nothing. I think we need to be careful, though. Leon will be coming for us. Let's go find Sam and see how Bethany is doing."

A quick dart across the dusk laden sky, and they were at the office of Dominique Dunworthy.

Amry knocked on the closed door and they waited for a reply.

"Who is it?"

"It's us, Miss Dunworthy. Ophelia and Amry."

"Oh girls, come in." She sang out.

Bethany lay on a plush, red sofa, covered from neck to toe in an opalescent, tissue thin blanket. Sam knelt beside her, holding her hand, and whispering in her ear.

"Will she be all right?" Ophelia floated, hovering above them.

"She will. Sam got her here just in time. Her energy was nearly drained beyond repair. But my vitality blanket will restore her essence. Bethany will be re-energized in a few hours. Now, how about telling me what happened to cause this? Mr. Burkletter seems less than forthcoming when I asked for an explanation." Ms. Dunworthy furrowed her brow.

Ophelia caught Sam's stare and they both turned to Amry.

The group chose silence.

"Okay. I see we're not going to get anywhere with this. But remember kids, you can talk to me about anything. I'm only here to help. Whatever, or whoever did this, it was very dangerous, and nearly cost Bethany her existence. Please, don't try to handle this on your own." Ms. Dunworthy smiled gently.

Ophelia nodded. Floating beside Amry, the two girls collapsed on the carpet next to their friends.

THE HUMAN SIDE OF OPHELIA

The sunset projected a kaleidoscope of orange, gold and a hit of pink across the western hemisphere. Ophelia gasped at the beauty. She never grew tired of it.

The events of the day before had worn her out completely. She laid her head down on the pillow at 11 p.m. and didn't open her eyes until 10 o'clock that morning. Curling the blanket around her folded body, the open window held her gaze.

A few hours of silence and exhaustion wore them down last night. Ophelia and Amry finally explained to Miss Dunworthy what had happened, holding back the part about the book. She sent the girls back to their room to rejuvenate and alerted the security team.

Bethany had been doing much better when she and Amry left. Sam was going to stay with her through the night; he was worried Leon might attempt to enact revenge. Miss Dunworthy assured him that Mr. Coal and Mr. Rain had been alerted—they sent out a team to search for him.

Ophelia lifted her head; Amry wasn't in the room. Rolling

over, she peeled back the blanket, and slid onto the floor. Gliding to the window, she spotted her friend walking toward the dorm.

"Hey. Where did you go?" Ophelia called out.

Amry waved. "I'll be up in a second."

Floating to the bathroom, Ophelia turned on the shower and stood under a stream of cool water. She needed the chill to snap her out of the grogginess. *I can't believe I slept for eleven hours.* She mumbled to herself.

Amry knocked on the door. "Lia? You in the shower?"

"Yes. I'm almost done."

By the time she stepped from the stall to the mirror, her hair was dry. The perk of being a celestial, and just another question to add to the long list she already had. Gazing at her reflection, her chest sawed an uneven heave. *This was it. Who she'd be for eternity. No aging, no family of her own. Her life had barely begun.* Most of the time Ophelia tried not to contemplate the what ifs. It's painful and pointless. But last night, when Roger came so close to banishing Bethany's soul to *The Nowhere,* the mortality of life and death became one. She had been taught in Sunday school that after you die, no worries of the living world followed you. But now she knew the truth. There's an end of sorts to everything—even death. Whether it's taking your last breath, or an eternity wandering in darkness, your state of being is stolen away.

Haven pushed through the self-pity in her head. It had been so long since she'd heard anything new about her little sister. Then, out of the blue pops a breather. *Who is this Alex McKenna? How can he help her little sister?*

"Lia, what the heck are you doing in there?"

"I'm coming."

Ophelia opened the door.

"I was beginning to think you fell into a vortex. After last night, I'm not second guessing anything." Amry tapped her fingers on the bed.

"Is everything all right? You seem agitated." Ophelia hovered by the bed.

"Not agitated. Well, maybe a little. But mostly pissed. They haven't found Leon yet. The khaki twins have been searching all night. Dictator Dick canceled all Saturday morning activities. We're supposed to stay in our rooms, but that's a bust. Half the school is in the courtyard. You ready to go?"

"Sure. Where are we going?"

"Check on Bethany and Sam, then maybe a little research. Do you have the book?"

Ophelia slid it out from under her pillow.

"I have it. But I think we should leave it here." Ophelia clutched the book. "What if someone sees it, like Ms. Dunworthy? Or the khaki twins?"

"You're right. We'll go get Sam and Bethany and come back here. We're supposed to be in our rooms anyway. Damn." Amry peered out the window.

"What is it?"

"Zachary." Amry sighed, "We haven't been watching him."

"You go to Bethany and Sam. I will go look for our project and see what he is up to. We can meet back here."

Ophelia checked the courtyard first, then the library, and finally, the North Tower. It was a popular place for kids to go when they needed time to themselves. The largest of all the towers on campus, it was constructed with a look out point that circled the entire structure. Zachary wasn't there.

Trying to avoid the only place she hadn't checked, Ophelia gave in and found herself standing in front of Zachary's dorm

room. Pressing her ear up to the door, she heard movement. Fist to oak, she knocked twice.

"What is it?" Zachary snapped.

"It's Ophelia."

"Oh. Abomination ... What do you want?"

Ophelia was startled by the abrupt opening of the door. "I said, What. Do. You. Want?" "Uh ..."

Ophelia panicked. She hadn't thought this through. *Idiot.* She whispered under her breath.

"What did you say? Did you just call me an idiot?"

Zachary hovered so close; Ophelia shuddered.

"By God's bones, what is that?" Zachary scowled.

"What is what?"

"Look at your arm."

Ophelia glanced down at her arms; the hairs were standing up.

"Never mind. What are you doing?"

"I am settling in for afternoon tea, is it not obvious?"

"Must you always be so obnoxious?"

"Must you always be so strange?"

Ophelia sized him up. He never met her eyes. Cocking her head, she directed her gaze to the room. The sheets on the bed were mussed and his pillow was squished between the wall and the mattress.

"You know for someone accusing me of being strange, you seem very familiar with your bed."

Zachary looked over his shoulder at the roughed-up sheets. "Which means?"

"Everyone knows celestials don't sleep, except for me of course. Why is your bed unkept?"

"Because there's nothing to do in this god forsaken place, and I was laying down recharging. Is that a crime?"

"Nope. But why lay down? Why not float? Or hover? Why choose the breather thing to do?"

If a celestial could change color, Ophelia swore Zachary would be fire engine red right about now. His nostrils flared, eyebrows scrunched, and his eyes widen twice their size. And yet, something gnawed at her. He was a contradiction. Laying in the comfort of one's bed, covering up in the covers and nestling to a pillow. Those were actions connected with human emotions. Usually, loneliness.

"Breather?" Zachary asked.

"A name Amry came up with for the living. I kind of like it."

"The whole lot of you are lunatics."

"Yes, well judging by your room, so are you," Ophelia snapped.

"Take that back. I swear if you say anything ..."

"You will what? Kill me? Amry was right, we should just tell your uncle you are hopeless."

Zachary inched backward. Lowering his head, he turned away from her.

"Tell my uncle whatever you wish, it will not make a difference. The end is inevitable. If you are finished here, shut the door."

Ophelia waved her hand inward and the door shut. Something felt off, he was different. Yes, he insulted her. Yes, he was a complete jerk. And yet, there was an air of vulnerability she hadn't seen in him before. Her instinct told her to not invade his space.

Whatever it was, she found him. Now she could join her friends.

By the time Ophelia reached Ms. Dunworthy's office, the gang was waiting for her outside on a grassy patch below the office window.

"Did you find Zachary?" Amry stood.

"I did. He's tucked safely in his room."

"Thank the universe." Amry smiled. "Let's go back to our room and check out the book."

The group clasped hands and teleported to the dorm. Breaking the rules was becoming a habit.

They all plopped on top of Ophelia's bed. She had the book opened to the page marked by Leon and Roger.

"What I can't figure out is, how did they open the portal?" Amry questioned.

"What do you mean?" Bethany blinked.

"In order to open the gateway to *The Nowhere*, you have to be a sorcerer. Also, to open any gateway to the in-between worlds, you have to have a sorcerer too. Roger wasn't a sorcerer, and neither is Leon."

"So how did they do it?" Ophelia curled her lip.

"We better find out, otherwise we're in deep shit." Sam stood.

"Let's take a look at some of the other chapters," Ophelia whispered.

"Lia. Why the mellow voice?" Amry chortled.

"I don't know. This all seems so mysterious."

"It sort of is, isn't it?"

Ophelia shook her head in agreement.

"Okay then," Amry whispered.

Ophelia grinned.

"The incantation is marked in red. Leon or Roger must have done that. However, when I flipped forward a few chapters, there's this." Ophelia pointed to the page.

Written in green on the left margin of the page was a poem.

One to open, one to close, to do it again, no one knows. For one soul the course is true, darkness comes, it's different for you. One to close, the deed is done, never ending, The Nowhere won.

"Uh, what the hell does this mean? The deed is done. *The Nowhere* wins?" Sam stuttered.

"It means, we keep this book a little while longer. We have questions and maybe this darn thing can answer them," answered Ophelia.

"Take charge, Lia." Amry grinned.

"Does everyone agree?" Ophelia asked.

"Agreed," they said in unison.

Further reading uncovered specific spells to get a soul to the in-between realms. You could accidentally cross into an open gateway, otherwise, only a sorcerer could gain access. It wasn't just the execution of words, but it was the magick needed to travel. There were twenty-eight known, in-between realms. Each needing its own incantation to navigate there. Opting into an in-between without the sorcerer by your side was ill advised. The realms could be tricky and deceiving, trapping you.

"This book mostly describes the in-betweens. There's very little about, *The Nowhere,*" Ophelia muttered.

"Maybe that's because no one knows. I mean think about it. Once you're banished, there's almost no coming back. How could anyone possibly have any details?" Amry rolled her eyes.

"She's right." Sam agreed.

"Yeah, she is," Bethany chimed in.

"Do you agree with everything he says?" Ophelia complained.

"What?" Bethany's lip quivered.

"Nothing. I'm sorry Bethany. Forgive me?" Ophelia pleaded.

Bethany reluctantly shook her head.

Ophelia hated herself for talking to her friend like that. The pressure of Leon and Roger combined with Haven and now the breather, Alex McKenna, was overwhelming her. Oh, and not to forget the icing on the cake, their little project, Zachary.

"Nuts. We've been here all day. Maybe we should go check on Zachary," Ophelia suggested.

"I think you're right," Amry interjected.

They decided to stay together. Making the usual rounds,

and turning up empty handed, Ophelia suggested the movie theater.

Located at the north end of the campus just before the Headmaster's private cottage, it was the place where aspirations still existed, and Ophelia's other favorite escape. Nothing could beat the possibilities that books created, but this was definitely a close second. Maybe Zachary felt the same way. After all, as much as he complained about the library, he seems to spend a lot of time there.

The Headmaster had ordered everyone back to their normal schedules. Leon was still out there, but he was not having his school paralyzed by one sour soul. Since the arrival of reinforcements, the security team was everywhere. A perk about being the Headmaster, he knew people.

The theater was nearly empty. There was a cartoon playing. Something Ophelia recognized from the last movie they had seen. Hovering from a bird's eye view, she spotted Zachary on the right side, about halfway down the theater. Pointing to him, the group followed her down and took a seat behind him.

Ophelia leaned in and expelled a long breath in his ear. Startled, Zachary jumped out of his seat.

Laughing, she sat back. He didn't scare her anymore. She wasn't sure why, he just didn't.

Zachary looked down, fuming.

"A stranger girl never I knew. You are ..."

"I'm what?"

"You are lucky that I am not in the mood." Zachary scowled.

"Just shut up and come back to your seat."

Zachary migrated to the center of the theater and sat.

The four followed him.

"What is wrong with all of you? Why don't you leave me alone?" Zachary demanded.

"You know why. Besides, it's been a long time since we've all seen a movie. How about we stay? What do you guys think?" Ophelia grinned.

"Sounds like a plan, Stan," Sam chuckled.

"Wonderful." Zachary replied sarcastically.

While the group hunkered down in the seats, Ophelia floated on a pocket of air in the center row. Eye level with the screen and submerged in the characters, she soaked up every bit of dialogue. She had only seen one movie before that car took her future, and it was only a short black and white documentary on the blizzards in New York City.

This was so much more. She was completely enamored with anything Hollywood. Ophelia swore that if her life hadn't been taken so abruptly, she would have been an actress like Mary Pickford. She wasn't much bigger than the actress and who knew? Maybe *she* would have been America's darling.

Ophelia peered down at her friends and the delinquent in their charge. She felt differently than when they first met Zachary. As if he were hiding himself. He talked like he was a criminal, but his actions didn't back up his words. Since he had gotten to the Academy, he'd pretty much kept himself. Maybe there was more to Zachary Kowal than he let them see.

Amry waved for her to come down, but Ophelia just nodded. She was where she wanted to be. The film was a comedy from the late nineties, *Galaxy Quest*. About a group of actors starring in a television series where they portray space travelers. The funny part begins when it happens to them in real life. Ophelia had found it hilarious, although she didn't quite understand all of it. She preferred the silent films herself.

Lying back, her body glided on the tracks of air, swaying her slightly. The opulent decor surrounding her cushioned the part of life she missed. Her soul soaked in the majesty of a world that had passed her by. The stories she watched on screen, and heard from recent students, were nothing like the time she knew. Modern. Contemporary. Urban.

Walking through a mall, playing with an iPhone, and the deliciousness of fast food.

Her thoughts clouded her mind, robbing her of the peace she had felt moments ago. Reminding her of experiences she would never know.

Shaking it off, she pulled herself back to the present. Ophelia hadn't noticed when the stranger seated next to Amry arrived. They were engaged in conversation. An older gentleman wearing a black suit and a white shirt with a long gray beard draping over the collar and nestling on his round belly. He leaned close and whispered furiously. Straining her neck to get a better look at the man, an Amish style hat hid most of his face. Abruptly, they ended their talk and he left.

"Lia. Can you come down here for a minute?" Amry called. Ophelia sat up and floated down to an empty seat next to her.

"Everything all right?" Ophelia whispered.

"Yeah. I had a question for you. When Haven ran out into the street to get the ball, where were you?"

"What? Why are you asking me this? You know where I was," Ophelia snapped.

"The porch, right?"

"Yes."

"You heard the horn, saw the car and ran out to Haven, right?"

"Indeed. What is going on? Why are you bringing this up?" Ophelia pursed her lips.

"I need to be sure I got the facts right," Amry replied.

"The facts right for what? Enough of this secrecy, tell me now," Ophelia raised her voice.

"Will you two take it outside, we're trying to watch the movie," Sam scolded.

"Okay Lia, let's go to the lobby."

The two girls whisked up toward the ceiling and whooshed into the lobby. Ophelia sat on the bottom step of the staircase leading to the balcony.

"Amry, I don't know what you are doing, but stop. You of all people know how badly this upsets me. I haven't heard any new information about the Soul Gatherer or Haven in months. Bringing up that day just makes it worse," Ophelia pleaded.

"I'm sorry, Lia. I know it's painful. But I was trying to help you."

"Help me, how? And who was that man you were talking to?" "His name is Albert Johnson. He's been here awhile. Refuses to cross over. Says he can do better by sticking around. I heard about him from one of the other teachers. That is, I heard one of the teachers talking about him. I tracked him down yesterday. This was our first meeting."

"And what was it you wanted from him?"

"Two things, actually. First, to find out if he knew anything about Haven and the Soul Gatherer."

"Does he?" Ophelia scooted closer.

"He's gonna work on it. Says he knows who we're talking about. The Soul Gatherer has been around a long time, way before Mr. Johnson got here. He has a contact he can speak to.

He'll get back to us in a few days." Amry rubbed Ophelia's shoulder.

"And the second thing?"

"Um, that's the one I wanted to find out for you, but also for all of us." Amry wriggled.

"Just say it. You are making my stomach ball up in knots." Ophelia rubbed her belly.

"That."

"That what?"

"The thing you just did. Rubbing your stomach like it hurts."

"It does hurt." Ophelia knitted her brow.

"I know. But why does it hurt?"

"I just told you ..."

"No. Why do you feel pain? Warmth? The need to sleep. None of us have experienced anything other than the energy drainage from making ourselves solid for too long. Why can you do this? I know it bugs you. And it confuses us. I thought it was time we got some solid answers. Headmaster Abernathy continues to brush it off. Tells us he'll investigate it, but I think he already knows and doesn't want to say. That's why I asked Mr. Johnson to help. But I wanted to be sure the facts I gave him were correct." Amry leaned into Ophelia.

"You know they are," Ophelia spoke in a small voice.

"I do. But this had to be accurate, so we could get answers. I was just fact checking. Hey, I thought you'd be excited?"

"I am. It's just, I don't know if I want to hear the answer. What if it's something creepy?"

"Something creepy?" Amry laughed, "We're already dead, how much creepier can we get?"

Ophelia giggled. All the tension she felt a moment ago, vanished. Amry was right. No matter the explanation, it didn't really matter. She was celestial and there was no coming back from that.

A surge of electricity raced through her pseudo veins once she allowed the thought to take hold.

Maybe I will finally find out why I am different. And Haven ... she felt lightheaded.

Amry continued, "He told me the Soul Gatherer has been here forever. Like the beginning. No one knows what happened to him and why he won't cross. But he's fondest of the children. Maybe something happened to his own kids or something. I don't know. Hopefully, Mr. Johnson will be able to help you find Haven."

"I miss her so much. The thought that she is out there alone sickens me. Our parents don't know what happened to us. If I can find Haven, we can be reunited." Ophelia's eyes sparkled.

"I know. It'll be a happy, and sad day." Amry looked away.

"What is wrong?" Ophelia was confused.

"You'll be gone. I'll be alone."

"No, you won't. You'll still have Sam and Bethany. Besides, maybe if I'm gone, you'll figure out why you're still here. Then we can be together on the other side. You will see your family again, too."

Ophelia tried to soothe her friend. It hurt her, too. The thought of never seeing Amry again tore her up.

"You're right. The whole thing is so weird, though. You'd think after all these years, I'd get used to the dead thing. But the truth is, most of the time I'm clueless. I just put up a good front. I do miss my family, but I've never spent too much time on the why. I just knew I was here." Amry frowned.

"We'll figure this out. Thank you for trying to find Haven. And, also for me. I wish I knew you when I was alive." Ophelia hugged Amry.

"Yeah, me too. Although, by the time I was born, you'd be really old." Amry grinned.

"Details." Ophelia smiled. "So, where do we go from here?"

"We wait."

"What about Alex? I think he's important to all of this." Ophelia fidgeted with her hands.

"I need to tell Mr. Johnson. Maybe he knows something about Alex McKenna."

"No, don't say anything. Please. Let Mr. Johnson find out what he can and, in the meantime, I'm going wait for the portal to open again. And this time, I'll be ready with questions."

"Okay Lia, however, you want to do this. I'm in." Amry hugged her.

The girls went back into the theater after a promise of keeping this to themselves until they had more information.

Ophelia levitated back to her comfort spot, taking with her the newly found feeling of hope. Letting out a heavy sigh, she quieted the traffic in her head and let the movie shove out all the questions. There would be plenty of those over the next few days. For now, she needed to laugh.

CAIN AMRY THEARIGE COMPANY

Two days had passed since Amry had told Ophelia about Mr. Johnson, and the quest to find Haven. The waiting was the worst, no matter how many questions she had for Amry, there were no answers yet.

It was Sunday evening and Monday classes had been canceled. The teachers were off to a yearly council meeting to discuss the curriculum for the new year. Or at least that's what they told the students. Ophelia felt there was more to it, but there was no evidence of this assumption, only her gut interfering with her brain. She decided to settle in and read a new book, *77 Shadow Street* by Dean Koontz. He had become her favorite author in death. Books had drastically changed over the past one hundred eight years, and she for one, loved it.

A trickle of chills ran up the cavity that once held her spine, and her hands ached from the night air. Closing the window, she decided a hot shower would melt away the beginning of spring, which, in the evening, offered a complete contrast to the seventy plus degrees of the day. Apparently, she wasn't the only one to feel the angst of the living. Someone needed to tell the Academy it operated in the world of the dead and stop the seasonal changes. But then again ... why were there showers? She quickly dismissed the thought. It didn't matter, she was happy they were there.

Stepping into the water, she closed her eyes and let her energy drink up the relaxing calm of security. Peace flooded her overactive thoughts, and the vision of white sheets bellowing in a soft breeze succeeded in completing the harmony. When she was sure the events from the past few days had been securely locked away, she eased down the lever, reducing the waterfall to a trickle, and then a memory.

Wrapped in a plush pale pink robe, she pulled the comforter down on her bed and wriggled underneath the covers. Fluffing her pillow, she propped it up against the wall and enjoyed the moment. Since you only receive one outfit upon arrival to your beginning, having the comfort of a warm robe was an exception the Headmaster made just for Ophelia. He told her it was a gift to make her time at the Academy more comfortable. Ophelia knew it was because she was the only celestial to take showers.

Closing her eyes, Ophelia could still picture her bedroom in the house she had loved so much. A large, oak dresser with matching mirror captured the eye as you walked into her room. Her mother had a huge, paisley patterned area rug placed under her four-poster bed for the cold winter mornings. A gold, brocade comforter with tiny, brown flowers was the main attraction. It had been ordered from Paris and took several months to arrive. Ophelia adored the lush, plump feeling as it draped over her at night.

Opening her eyes, she squirmed further down, tucking the comforter under her chin. Inhaling the scent of print to paper, she turned the page to the first chapter.

Bam! The door flung open, slamming into the wall. Startled, Ophelia shot up, dropping her book on the floor.

"Lia!" Amry's voice was penetrating.

"What is going on?" Ophelia tensed up.

"You need to get dressed. Now." Amry pulled out a dress from Ophelia's side of the closet.

"What's wrong? You're scaring me." Ophelia slid into her mid-length dress and snatched a sweater from Amry's hand.

"I'm sorry, but we have to go."

"Where are we going?"

"Sam and Bethany are waiting for us downstairs. Headmaster wants us to take Zachary and hide in the in-between."

"What?" Ophelia's eyes widened.

"I'll explain later, promise. No time for privacy and closed doors. Grab my hand!"

One step through the wall and they were in the lobby with Sam and Bethany.

"Where's Zachary?" Ophelia spun around searching the room.

"He's in the Headmaster's office. We're going there now." Amry took Ophelia's hand.

"Wait. Is Zachary in danger? Why the in-between?"

"Yes. And because the Headmaster said so," Amry stated.

"Oh great. That clears it all up," Ophelia said sarcastically.

Amry furrowed her brow and tightened her grip on Ophelia's hand. Two steps forward placed them in the office of Headmaster Abernathy. Zachary was standing in the middle of the room surrounded by the sorcerer twins, Mr. Coal and Mr. Rain, Dictator Dick, and Abernathy himself.

"All of you, hurry up," the Headmaster insisted.

Zachary's face had lost all poise. His fear filled the room, drawing each one of them closer to console him. Ophelia's heart cavity mimicked a manic pounding as if the organ still lay nestled in her chest. She clenched her fist to her breastbone to quiet the thumping seizing her ears.

"Miss Wetherton, are you all right?" Dictator Dick glared.

"I'm fine. Don't worry about me," Ophelia snapped.

"I need the four of you to take my nephew to the *Now* and stay there until you get word from me that it's safe." Abernathy hustled them all into a circle.

"Safe from what?" Sam asked.

"Mr. Burkletter there isn't time. I promise to explain when you return." Abernathy opened a small book.

Ophelia recognized it. A duplicate to the one under her pillow.

"And the students here?" Ophelia frowned.

"They'll be fine."

"I don't understand. What exactly is this place?" Ophelia's swiped her hands on her dress.

"Miss Wetherton, we don't have time for this. You will see soon enough."

Abernathy raised his hands and commanded. "Not here, not there, not anywhere. Through the door I vow, to the realm which is Now."

Ophelia gasped as the blackness crept down the walls of the room and cloaked them in darkness. Amry whispered words of comfort in her ear, but they did little to ease her apprehension. The Headmaster's voice grew further and further away as the blackness coddled their bodies and lifted them weightless in the atmosphere.

Ophelia shut her eyes tight. The movement made her dizzy. She pushed back the churning nausea with her throat muscles, holding the sour taste of bile at bay. She hoped Amry would hear from Mr. Johnson when they got back ... *if* they got back. The idea of tasting and feeling something that has been gone over a hundred years was beginning to freak her out. A hot shower was one thing, but phantom organs giving real sensation—she needed answers.

"Lia, open your eyes. We're here."

Ophelia tapped her foot on solid ground and sighed.

"Come on you, open them," Amry laughed.

Ophelia peeled open her lids. In front of her lay a narrow path, winding and twisting into a gray abyss. To her left, a crisp, clear view of the Academy, and to her right, a picture-perfect vision of the little town where the breathers resided.

"This is so peculiar." She reached her hand out toward the school, the image blurred. "What is it?"

"The two worlds surround us and we're occupying the space that separates them. Sort of like a doorway. On one side your room, on the other, the dorm hallway. We're standing directly in the threshold." Amry grinned.

"Why are you grinning? This is not funny." Zachary's voice cracked.

"I think it's kind of funny," Amry replied, "We can see everything going on in both places, but they have no clue we're watching." Amry pointed in both directions.

Zachary clenched his fists. "I know what this is. Remember?"

Ophelia gulped. They had all forgotten, she was sure of it.

Zachary had been banished to an in-between for five hundred years.

"Zachary, we are sorry," Ophelia apologized.

"Don't!" Sam snapped, "Why should you apologize to him?"

"Because he knows firsthand what the in-between is."

"So what?" Sam's voice deepened.

"So, stop judging. We have no idea what he has really been through," Ophelia defended.

Zachary's neck whipped and turned to Ophelia.

"Can we move around here?" Ophelia asked.

"You can walk along the pathway, you can sit down, and you can lay down, but don't disrupt the wall that separates us. And don't wander too far. You don't know what's out there," Zachary replied.

Ophelia gently smiled.

"We will be fine if we stay in place," Zachary suggested.

Ophelia shuddered; crossing her legs, she collapsed to the ground. Facing the town, she yearned to be there. Stretching her neck to get a better look, it saddened and yet exhilarated her at the same time.

"You never told us what happened to you?" She turned to Zachary.

"My mother. She did not know my father was a sorcerer when they met. Worse, he practiced dark magick. By the time she found out, it was too late. He killed her. But she hid me with some friends. Unfortunately, he found the couple and killed them too. I was older by then and took to the streets, surviving anyway I could."

Ophelia was stunned.

"I am so sorry that happened to you. I could never imagine my parents ever doing anything to harm me or Haven." Ophelia skipped a breath.

"Yeah, dude. That's the worst," Sam chimed in.

Bethany and Amry nodded in agreement.

"Is your dad still trying to find you? Is that who you're hiding from?" Ophelia leaned closer.

"No. He's dead. It is who I am; that is why I'm being hunted. His followers want me because I am half dark sorcerer."

A bolt of light pierced through the darkness and swirled its way toward them creating a circular motion above their heads.

The vision of town blurred into the blackness, filling the crevices of open space. Swaying with weightlessness once again, Ophelia's stomach soured. In a moment they were back in the Headmaster's office.

"Children, is everyone all right?" Abernathy cleared his throat.

"We are well, uncle," Zachary acknowledged.

"We need answers." The four of them ganged up on Abernathy.

"As I promised. There are souls who wish to take my nephew and use him for evil. Things that would affect both the world of the living and the dead. They want to control his dark side. His father was very powerful, but just as malevolent. My poor sister didn't realize any of this until it was too late, the price was her life. Most of what you read about Zachary is false. A cover made up to get him to the Academy. They couldn't know he was my nephew." Abernathy sat.

"He wasn't banished to the in-between?" Ophelia asked.

"No, he was. But it was to save his soul. I sent him there for a short time. I had no idea that Zachary would fall prey to the Underworld."

"Wait. I thought that is what the Academy was?" Ophelia inquired.

"No, Miss Wetherton. The world of the Academy is occupying the same space as the living."

"What?" All four students clamored to Abernathy.

"Uncle, please explain." Zachary's eyes widened.

"When I created this for all of you, it was not its only purpose. I knew one day I would find Zachary. And when I did, I would need a safe place to bring him. Creating a new realm attracts a lot of unwanted attention. So instead, I used an existing school. A veil between us keeps the worlds separated."

"That's why there are showers, and the gym, and the cafeteria," Ophelia gasped.

"Precisely. Although I must say it's worked out for you my dear girl," Abernathy chuckled.

"What school?" Ophelia squeaked.

"Excuse me?"

"What is the name of the school that we are sharing? It would be different than The Academy of Souls."

"Cain Amry Thearige Academy."

"I'm sorry, what did you say?" Amry squinted.

"I'm not sure I understand the question. Do you have trouble hearing, Miss Goodman?"

"No. You said, Cain Amry Thearige Academy, yes?"

"Indeed."

"That's my great, great grandfather. I was named after him."

"So, you're actually in the school named after a member of your family?"

Sam chimed, "Cool."

"Yes." Amry stared out the window.

"Headmaster. Where is the other academy located?" Ophelia inquired.

"The original building was constructed in England several hundred years ago, but we share worlds with a replica created in America some one hundred plus years ago. Thearige's grandson wanted the exact duplicate. He had several bricks taken from a tower no longer in use and transported across the ocean. His academy is a monument to his great grandfather who created a small village in Floral Park, New York."

"And Amry is connected to all of this," Ophelia murmured.

"Did you know?" Amry glared at Abernathy.

"No, Miss Goodman. I promise you; I had no idea."

"What difference does it make? Can we get back to Zachary and why we had to go to the in-between? Which, by the way is creepy as shit," Sam demanded.

"Yes. The souls that want him will stop at nothing."

"And they were here at the school?" Sam interrogated.

"Not at the school. They were lurking about in town. But I fear if they get too close, they will uncover the veil. Then both schools will be in jeopardy."

"You're a sorcerer, why don't you just get rid of them?" Sam huffed.

"There are too many of them. If I strike at one group, another will just take their place. I'm trying to find a way to reach all of them, I just need more time." Abernathy dropped his chin.

"I have a question," Ophelia asked.

"Yes, Miss Wetherton." Abernathy raised his head.

"Not you. Him." Ophelia pointed to Zachary. "Why were you such a bastard when you arrived here?" Ophelia furrowed her brow.

"I thought it'd be safer for everyone else if they stayed away from me. I did not plan on my uncle having the four of you babysit me." Zachary glared at Abernathy.

Headmaster Abernathy cleared his throat.

"Now all of you understand the entire situation. Please keep this to yourselves. The least number of students who know, the better. Mr. Coal and Mr. Rain will discreetly be following all five of you. Stay together but keep up appearances. If Zachary blends in, the better it will be for his safety, the living, and the dead."

No one had any words left. They just nodded.

Needing some time to discuss what had happened and the new introduction to who Zachary really is, they had agreed to meet at the library.

Ophelia needed to recharge. Somehow, having human tendencies wore her energy down quicker than her friends. Promising to join them shortly, she went back to the dorm room to lie down. An hour of rest would be enough to regain her full strength.

Snuggling her pillow, she rolled onto her side facing the room. Amry's bed was perfect as usual. Which wasn't difficult, she rarely laid on it. A small circle of light hovered above the neatly folded blanket at the foot of the bed. She glanced out of the window at the sliver of sky peeking out—dusk. The sun had nearly set. Lifting her head, she widened her eyes. The sphere appeared bigger than a moment ago. Shooting up, she clutched her pillow to her chest and gasped as it ferociously spun in a circular motion creating a screeching wind. Ophelia dropped her pillow and covered her ears. It was happening again, this time, she'd be ready.

WELCOME TO THE ACADEMY
ALEX MCKENNA

The chiming of the doorbell signaled dinner had arrived. Alex slipped his debit card out of his wallet and gave the delivery girl a generous tip with payment. His mom had been a waitress in her younger days and schooled both her kids on showing appreciation for a job well done. Working to get her real estate license, she relied on tips to get her through school.

Margaret poured them each a glass of soda, grabbed some napkins and paper plates from the kitchen cabinet, and followed Alex up the staircase to his room. Although the house was empty, they both preferred the sanctuary of his bedroom. It was theirs. The one domain in the house they didn't have to share.

Plopping down on the bed next to each other, Alex lay the pizza box on his lap and opened it. Garlic, pepper, and melted mozzarella pervaded through the air and nestled on the inhale, filling his nose with an explosion that ignited his taste buds and made his mouth water.

"Mmm, cheese paper," Margaret cooed.

She reached in and stretched off a piece of melted cheese from the wax paper below the pie.

"You know, Lorenzo's is one of the few pizzerias' that still puts that paper in the box." Alex observed.

"I know. That's why I love it so much." Margaret pulled off another wayward glob of cheese.

"And that's why I love you so much."

"Because I like cheese paper?" She licked her lips.

"The simplest things are so exciting to you. Most people could care less about cheese that's melted into wax paper, but you, it's a fascination. And that fascinates me." He leaned in and peppered her neck with kisses.

"Maybe after our pizza, we should think about dessert," Margaret said coyly.

"Oh, there's no maybe. We are definitely having some dessert."

ALEX SLIPPED his arm out from underneath Margaret's neck. They had fallen asleep and the TV was still on. He reached for the remote on the nightstand and clicked it off. Silently stretching, he nearly fell when his socks slid across the oak floor. A quick look at Margaret, she was still sleeping peacefully. He quietly padded across the room and ambled down to the kitchen.

Pouring a glass of soda, he sat at the table. Peering out of the sliding glass doors to the backyard, he could see the row of houses cascading down the block. His mom had opted not to fence in the yard but trim it with hedges, leaving the driveway to the garage bare. A perfect viewing platform for the rest of the neighborhood behind them.

The streetlamps illuminated the black empty sea of asphalt.

A quiet calm laced the row of sleepy houses. Alex reveled in the tranquility. So much noise constantly filling his head, any semblance of stillness wrapped around his mind like a child's favorite blanket.

In the center of the glass, a small sphere of light caught his attention. At first, he thought it was in the yard. Leaning forward and squinting, he realized it was a reflection coming from directly behind him.

Jumping up, he spun around. Growing in diameter, it was beginning to spin.

"Hey, whatcha' doin'?" Margaret said groggily.

"Stop. Babe, slowly move to your left and come over here by me."

"Why? What's going on?"

Margaret gingerly slid to the left as Alex instructed, and then quickly scurried by his side. "What do you see?"

"It's the vortex opening, the gateway to that girl, Ophelia."

"Alex, please be careful. Remember what your Gram said.

"Don't get too close," Margaret pleaded.

"She's there, it looks like a bedroom."

"What's she doing?"

"Sitting on the bed, she's covering her ears."

The wind whipped around the vortex howling like a wolf speaking to the full moon.

"I don't hear anything?" Margaret turned to Alex.

"It's like a high-pitched howl. It's deafening. Wait. It's quieting down. She sees me."

"What's she doing now?"

"She's coming closer."

Alex leaned closer to the anomaly.

"Alex, back up." Margaret tugged at his T-shirt.

"Babe. I gotta do this. Please. Let go of my shirt."

Margaret reluctantly let the fabric fall from her fingertips.

Alex inched closer.

"You are Alex McKenna, right?" Ophelia asked. The anxious teen widened her eyes in anticipation.

"Yes. I've seen Haven. Who is she?"

"She is my sister."

"I think she's in trouble," said Alex.

Ophelia floated off the bed and stood directly in front of the entrance to the living.

"I've been searching for her for years. She was taken by a man, a Soul Gatherer. I think she is counting on you to help."

"I think she is, too."

"Can you?" Ophelia's eyes widened.

"I can try. Where are you? Is it The Academy of Souls?"

Ophelia's chin dropped. "Yes. You know about my school?"

"I do."

"Oh no."

"What is it?'

"The gateway. It's closing!" Ophelia shouted.

Alex heard the desperation in her voice as he helplessly watched the circle shrink. The wind cried out once again, as it violently thrashed around the outer edges of the bridge between the dimensions.

"I have to go." Alex tasted Margaret's lips. "I'll be back soon."

"What the hell? No. Alex. You can't," Margaret shrieked.

"I love you," his voice trailed.

Alex stepped into the center of the storm. The vision of Ophelia rippled, traveling to the rim of the circle, and splashing into the void. "This shield is my power to protect against evil, this shield keeps out harm. No dark entities shall pass through this shield. As I will it, so shall it be."

Sawing to fill his lungs with air, he pushed forward and landed on the floor of the dorm room. Gazing up, Ophelia stood in front of him, her mouth wide open.

"Ugh. My head hurts. Where are we?" a voice echoed.

Alex winced. His heart punching the walls of his chest.

Whipping his head around in a frenzy, Margaret was lying on the floor beside him.

"No, no, no, no. What the fuck, *il mio amore?*" Alex scrambled to her side.

Ophelia moved closer. With her pointer finger, she quickly poked his shoulder and retracted.

Alex didn't respond. His focus was Margaret.

"How could you do this? *Why* did you do this?" his voice strained.

"I couldn't let you go without me."

Alex kissed away the saltiness from her cheeks. With the back of his sleeve, he gently patted dry her eyes.

"Alex?" Ophelia murmured.

The couple turned to the bewildered Ophelia Wetherton. They were abruptly interrupted by three harsh wraps on the door."

Miss Wetherton, is everything all right in there?' Dictator Dick shouted.

"Yes, Mr. Cander. I'm fine." She drew her pointer finger to her mouth, alerting Alex and Margaret to keep quiet.

"We've registered an atmospheric disturbance coming from this room. Open the door, please."

"One second, I was in the shower."

Ophelia could hear another voice; someone was with the annoying guardian.

"The shower?" The unknown voice was raspy.

"This is that weird kid. The one I told you about," Dictator Dick explained.

"Oh. Yeah, that's right."

Ophelia fluttered her hand toward the bathroom. Alex and Margaret quickly scurried in as she closed the door after them.

"I'm coming. I needed to dress," Ophelia called out.

Standing in front of the door, Ophelia composed herself before turning the knob.

"Mr. Cander, please come in."

She stepped aside for the two men to gain entrance. The other guy accompanying Dictator Dick was a short, older man. His hair and beard were snow white. Ophelia giggled.

"What's so funny Miss Wetherton?"

"He looks like Santa Claus." Ophelia covered her mouth. "This is Ralph, he's part of the new security team. Show him some respect."

"I'm sorry. Nice to meet you, Ralph." Ophelia forced a smile.

Ralph tipped his head.

She waved her arm in the air. "See, nothing. I'm not sure what you detected, but everything's quiet here."

Dictator Dick looked around and then headed straight for the bathroom. When his hand clasped the knob, Ophelia collapsed. He went rushing to her side. "Miss Wetherton, are you all right?"

He scooped her up and lay her on the bed.

"Ralph, go get Ms. Dunworthy."

"No. There's no need. I saw her this morning. She told me to rest. I have used too much energy with everything that happened last night."

"Yes, well that makes sense. Are you sure you don't want us to get her?"

"Thank you, but I'll be fine after I rest." She slipped under the blanket.

Dictator Dick glanced at the bathroom and then back at Ophelia.

"Okay then. Ralph let's get out of here and let the girl rest. Miss Wetherton, if you see or hear anything suspicious, please call us."

"I will, Mr. Cander."

After the door shut, Ophelia threw the covers off and vaulted to the bathroom door. She knocked lightly.

"Alex. It's okay to come out."

Ophelia stepped back as Alex and Margaret emerged from the bathroom. Her energy didn't have enough time to recharge, and she worried if her waves would bother them.

"I am sorry for my appearance. My spirit is drained, and I have not been able to rest."

Margaret couldn't take her eyes from the hovering spirit.

"Please do not be frightened," Ophelia pleaded.

"I'm not. We're not. I've just never ... I mean, Alex sees ghosts all the time. This is a first for me." Margaret half smiled.

Ophelia giggled.

"What's so funny?" Margaret knitted her brow.

"You said ghost. Only a breather would call me a ghost."

"A breather?"

"The living." Ophelia looked down.

"Well—that would be us," Margaret said sarcastically.

Alex intervened.

"Ophelia, why are you drained? Did something happen to you?"

Ophelia extended her hand to the bed, they took the cue and sat. Keeping a comfortable distance, she sat on Amry's bed.

Ophelia wasn't afraid of them, but she sensed Margaret might not feel the same.

"We had a horrible night with a bad soul. He kidnapped one of our friends, and in the end, he was thrown into, *The Nowhere.*"

"Is your friend okay?" Alex asked.

"She is. You didn't ask me what *The Nowhere,* was." Ophelia knitted her brows.

"You're sitting here with two breathers' in your world of the dead. The fact that Alex didn't ask about some nowhere place is what strikes you as odd?" Margaret narrowed her eyes.

"Are you angry with me?" Ophelia blinked.

Margaret's eyes widened. "No. I'm not angry. Just confused."

"Ophelia, please excuse Margaret's abruptness. She wasn't supposed to be here."

Alex glanced over at Margaret.

"What the hell were you thinking, babe?"

"I didn't want to lose you. We didn't know if you were gonna be able to make it back."

"And your solution was to join me?"

"Yeah, I know. Wasn't really thinking about the consequences."

Margaret stood and walked to Ophelia.

"I'm sorry for being bitchy. This is a little different than Alex's other cases."

"Cases?" Ophelia's body rippled.

"That's going to take some getting used to," Margaret proclaimed.

"Sorry."

"Don't be. It's different, but kind of cool." Margaret smiled. Alex interjected, "Ophelia, I see the dead. Which is why we were able to connect. I try to help them when they need it. Most of the time it's just finishing something so they can cross over. Although lately, they've been getting a lot harder."

"I'll say. His last case, there were five murders, two evil spirits ... well, one evil and one good spirit turned evil for a little while, a demon, and a crazy old bitch. It was intense." Margaret shook her head.

"Oh wow." Ophelia floated to the door.

Opening it a crack, she peered down the hallway, it was vacant. She gently closed the door.

"I need to tell my friends you are here. I think it would be best if the two of you stay in my room. I'll go and get them. Then we can tell you everything."

"About Haven?" Alex inquired.

"Yes. Haven and the rest of it."

"Wait. There's more?"

Alex's words fell upon deaf ears. Ophelia had already slipped through the door.

"Margaret. I'm so pissed right now."

"I know you are. I'm sorry. But after that last case, I couldn't let you go alone. I worry about you, and you're just gonna have to accept that I'm here."

"Do I have a choice?"

Margaret looked around the room.

"I'm thinking, nope."

"I wonder what's brought me here besides, Haven? I guess we'll find out soon enough."

"Babe. Come here and check this out."

Margaret was standing by the window. She had pulled back the right side of the curtain and was peering out to the courtyard. There were several teens floating to their destinations and a few hovering in the center of campus. Two celestials were sitting on the edge of the roof, feet dangling.

"Is this awesome or what?" Margaret exclaimed.

Alex laughed, "And this is why we belong together. Anyone else would have been totally freaked."

"Uh, I was freaked when we first landed in this weird, day of the dead place. But after talking with Ophelia, I feel calmer."

"Yeah. She does have that effect, doesn't she? There's something very different about her."

Alex sat at the end of the bed, soaking in the atmosphere. *A high school for the dead, and they were there. Wait until he told his Gram. He just might wind up here after he tells her, but the look on her face would be worth it.* He chuckled to himself.

Alex sniffed ozone. The kinetic energy in the air had the same result as a thunderstorm storm back home. All the celestials created an enormous amount of electricity. He looked down at the raging goosebumps on his arms, tiny hairs stood at attention.

Running his fingers along the wall, the stone felt damp. A blanket of familiarity brought peace.

"It's strange how comfortable this place feels." Alex glanced up at Margaret.

"I know what you mean. Aside from the levitating spirits, this reminds me so much of our school. But we don't have dorms."

"I don't think these are actual dorms. Look outside, this is the same view from our art class."

"Oh yeah. You're right." Margaret nodded.

"And think, art is the only class with its own bathroom."

"Cool. We should be able to navigate around here fairly easy.

If the campus is the same, we already know the lay of the land."

"Yup." Alex grinned.

Their conversation was interrupted when Ophelia and friends passed through the closed door.

Startled, Alex surged up from the bed.

"Do not be afraid." Ophelia pleaded.

"Oh, I'm not. Just taken off guard."

"We didn't want to draw attention and risk someone seeing you when we opened the door. The school is on alert trying to find Leon.

"Leon?" Alex raised a brow.

"I promised to tell you everything. If you take a seat, we'll explain. But first, I'd like to introduce you to my friends. Amry, Zachary, Bethany and Sam, this is Alex and Margaret."

Sam moved closer to Alex and locked eyes.

"The two of you are breathers, so how come you could see Ophelia when the gateway opened?'

"I could. Not Margaret. I see the dead. It's a family thing," said Alex.

"Oh jeez. Even in all this shit that's going on, you guys have to fling the testosterone. The both of you back off." Amry pulled Sam back.

"Alex. Really?" Margaret barked.

The two boys retreated.

Everyone took a seat on the bed, the floor, and whatever was available. Ophelia started the story with her beginning and the loss of Haven to the Soul Gatherer and finished up with Zachary fleeing from the group that wanted to make him their bitch. She filled in the spaces with Mr. Johnson, Roger's banishment to *The Nowhere,* and Leon's impending capture.

Alex listened intensely.

"I guess we need to tackle one problem at a time. Leon sounds like security's problem. We can all keep Bethany safe if we stay together. Zachary, pretty much the same thing. But Haven and the Soul Gatherer, I think that's our priority right now. I keep sensing we're running out of time."

"Me too," Ophelia blurted out, "I have never felt the urgency that I've experienced with the last few dreams. I'm convinced if we don't find her soon, her soul will be lost forever."

"I agree." Alex nodded.

"You left out a big piece of the story," Bethany murmured.

"What do you mean?" Alex inquired.

"Ophelia." Bethany pointed.

"Bethany! That is not important right now," Ophelia snapped.

"If I'm gonna help, I need to know everything. Ophelia?"

"Lia, tell him," Amry chimed.

Ophelia rose up and sliced through the air and out the window. A few seconds later she came back. Her chest heaved as she took a long breath and then blew.

Alex reached out to the faint trail of wind on his fingertips.

"How? What?" His eyes widened.

Amry stood and leaned into her friend.

"Lia can feel things and do things that mimic the living. No one else has ever had this capability. At least no one that Headmaster Abernathy has ever met. That's why we're in this dorm room. It has a shower. Lia loves her morning hot showers." Amry winked.

"Mr. Johnson is not only helping me find Haven, Amry asked him to find answers about me." Ophelia dropped her chin. "Do I frighten you?"

Alex and Margaret looked at each other and grinned.

"Nope," They answered in unison.

"Alex, maybe you should tell them a little about our past together. Especially your last case," Margaret suggested.

"First thing you should know, Margaret is probably the strongest breather you'll ever meet. She's been on some pretty tough cases with me, and she hasn't cracked yet." He grinned.

After the condensed history about the Russo/LaBoccetta bloodline and his immediate family, Alex explained to his captive audience about their last case—the Geranium deaths.

The ghostly teens were wide-eyed, hanging on every word as Alex described the five murders. He especially noticed Zachary when the mention of dark magick was brought up. The boy buried his face into crossed arms, tightening his body into a closed clam shell.

"That is why they want me. To raise the beasts, wreak havoc on the living, and help them open the Underworld in-between. They think they can own the realms," Zachary sighed.

"We won't let them, I promise. But first, Haven," Alex soothed.

"How were you able to get here?" Bethany asked.

"When the portal opened, I jumped through. I just didn't know I had a passenger." Alex glanced at Margaret.

"Yeah, whatever. Let's stop beating that dead horse."

"See, I told you she's fierce." He grinned.

"Amry, when are you meeting Mr. Johnson again?" Alex asked.

"Hopefully he'll have news for me tomorrow."

"I'd like to be there when you see him."

"I'm not so sure that's a good idea. We're trying to keep you two away from everyone. If Headmaster finds out, he'll more than likely send you back," Amry stated.

"We'll be okay. It would help if I could speak with him."

Amry reluctantly agreed.

"Ophelia, when did the dreams intensify?" Alex squinted.

"A few weeks ago."

"That's when I first started seeing Haven. I think we're both connected to her. I'm just not sure how yet."

"After you had your beginning, were you always been tied to the living?'

Ophelia nodded. "Since the moment I arrived at the Academy."

"Can you tell me about that day when you and Haven, what did you call it—started your beginning?"

Ophelia sighed. After one hundred plus years, it still gave her heartache to hear the details be recounted in her own words.

"I'm sorry if this is painful, but it helps. I promise."

Once again, Ophelia recounted the fateful day she lost her little sister and her life. The day her parent's lost both of their daughters. Hearing the words pass between her lips reminded her of how much she missed her family. The horror her parents felt when they arrived home must have been immeasurable. With each sentence, her breath became shallower. The wild pounding from a heart long gone pumped louder and louder, drumming its way to her inner ear. Ophelia's head spun as the room darkened and she billowed to the floor.

"Lia!" Amry rushed to her side.

"I think I know what to do," Alex instructed, "All of you lay a hand on Ophelia's body. Share your energy with her."

"What?" Sam's eyes widened.

"I know what you are doing, Alex. My uncle told me about this when I was a youngster." Zachary placed his hand on Ophelia's shoulder.

The rest of the gang followed his instructions and gently gripped Ophelia. In a few seconds, she was awake. Sitting up, she held her head.

"What happened?"

"You passed out," Alex said.

"Is that even possible?" Sam frowned.

Alex grinned. "She didn't lose consciousness like a breather.

Her energy was interrupted by grief. When you lay your hands on her, you jolted it back to a normal flow."

"How do you know this shit?" Sam said bitterly.

"Were you not listening when Alex told us the story about his family?" Amry huffed.

Sam rolled his eyes. "Doesn't mean he knows everything."

"Believe me Sam, I don't," Alex retorted.

"How you feeling, Lia? Is your head okay?" Amry curled her lip.

"I am much better."

"I'm so sorry I made you go through that," Alex apologized.

"It's all right. I know you are only trying to help."

His *spidey sense* was telling him it was more than want, he needed to help. He had a newfound urgency regarding Ophelia. *Why was this gnawing at him?* Alex closed his eyes.

His mind burned through the past and the history of his grandmother and grandfather told him about their family's experiences. A spirit being tethered to the living was strange, but Ophelia wasn't the first. He had forgotten about the tale of the halfway boy. The story in one of his Gram's journals. It took place in the Summer of 1822. A small village outside of Naples. The child was about seven, and like Ophelia, his little sister was playing in front of their home. A group of men on horses were traveling on a dirt road a few yards away from their property line. The sister ventured out after she saw them galloping towards the house. Enamored with the beautiful creatures, she ran straight for them. The men didn't see her until it was too late.

Grief stricken, the boy lost control. Blaming the horse for his sister's death, he began punching one of the steeds. Protecting itself, it reared up and crushed the boy. Only one child was supposed to be taken that day. Disrupting the natural order, the boy's soul became bound to the living world. Still feeling, yearning, and performing daily rituals in the afterlife. Two hundred years passed; his celestial being passing on the light every time it would offer peace. In the end, the little boy went mad and leaped through an open portal to a random in-between.

Ophelia has been refusing the gateway to cross over for a hundred years. Eventually her fate would mimic the boys. He needed to find Haven soon and bring her peace. He now had two souls to save.

He decided to wait to tell Ophelia the truth about her

oddities until he had more information that would confirm his beliefs.

"I'd like to see the campus," said Alex.

"Nooooo!" The gang replied.

"I get it. You're worried about us, and the Headmaster finding out. But I need to do this. I can't just sit and wait for something to happen. I want to go where Bethany was taken yesterday."

"There's nothing there. Just showers and a room at the end of the hall. We have the book here." Ophelia held up the prize.

"Book?"

"The one I told you about. Roger used it to open *The Nowhere.*"

Alex reached out and Ophelia released the book into his hands. Flipping through the pages, he gasped.

"What is wrong?" Ophelia's eyes widened.

"I've seen a book very similar to this."

Alex passed the book to Margaret.

"This looks like the one Greta had," Margaret replied. "That's what I thought. Flip to the middle of the book. Look at the picture drawn next to the spell."

Margaret's jaw dropped. It was the same incantation as the one that controlled Catherine, the unwilling murderess.

"Alex, what is going on?" Ophelia questioned.

"Remember the story about our last case? The book that Greta used to summon the spirit and control her? This is the spell she used." Alex pointed to the drawing. "I don't know how, but this book seems to be a duplicate of the one Greta had. Please, take us to the place where the portal to *The Nowhere* opened."

Ophelia looked at her friends. "Maybe if we teleported instead of walking them through campus?"

"We can't. Breathers can't travel that way." Amry frowned.

"If we stay solid, and together, we should do little to draw attention. We can walk, everyone knows Ophelia likes to stroll the campus most of the time. If we are with her, I do not think anyone will question it," Zachary surmised.

"What about their breath? The others will know," Ophelia replied.

"You are right. That could be a gapeseed. Over what span of time can you inhale?" Zachary asked.

"What?" Margaret quipped.

"How long can you go without taking in air?"

"I know what you mean. I just don't understand ... oh, I get it." Margaret glanced at Alex.

"You want us to walk across campus and not breath?" Alex shook his head.

"Not the entire journey. We will stop, you breathe, we go on. If we keep close to the hallways, we should be okay. Most of the kids are fliers." Zachary pointed to the window.

Alex nodded.

"What do you think?" He took Margaret's hand.

"We got this. After almost getting frozen to death, this will be a piece of cake." Margaret smirked.

"Okay, let's go." Alex paced toward the door.

"Wait!" Zachary called.

"Me, Amry, and Ophelia will go first. Then Alex and Margaret. Sam, you and Bethany protect them from the rear. I think this will appear to be the least conspicuous. The two lovers are normally distracted and lagging, whilst Amry and Ophelia are often engaged in conversation. As for myself, the entire school must know by now I am the unwilling ward of your ill-gotten position as my guardians.

"Will do," Sam smirked.

"Whatever you just said."

"If you are both ready, we will leave. Oh, and one more suggestion. If you should come across a haberdasher of nouns and pronouns, avoid looking into their eyes. They will know promptly you are imposters," stated Zachary.

"A haber—what?" Alex furrowed his brow.

"Pay no attention to the medieval gibberish Zachary spits out from time to time. He was a teenager during the 16th century when they spoke like they dressed—boring."

Zachary locked his teeth but ignored Amry's statement. "Take in a good breath before we open the door. Hold it until we are ready to go outside. When we pass through the doors to the courtyard, take in another breath. It is not that far to the west side hall. Once we are there, you should be able to breathe normally. Students rarely travel the halls. After that, it will be a longer walk through campus to the gym. Is this clear?"

"Yup." Alex clenched Margaret's hand.

The five friends materialized in solid form.

Filling his lungs, Alex squeezed Margaret's hand. They exchanged a glance and then relaxed. When the door closed behind them, Alex quivered. The electrical energy was intense. So many souls passing through the walls of the dorm, leaving traces everywhere they went. The charge raced through his veins, pumping a river of rapid blood to his heart.

"Babe, you're burning me," Margaret whispered.

Alex couldn't hear her. Buzzing in his ears had taken over, piercing the drum causing short bursts of pain. He needed to get to a desolate place as quickly as possible.

"Alex."

Margaret wriggled her hand, but his grip was too tight. The stronger the charge invading his body, the tighter he squeezed.

"Alex. Dude, let go," Margaret's voice carried.

"Margaret, what's wrong?" Ophelia murmured.

"It's Alex. Something's wrong. His hand is on fire and he won't let go. It's like he's not even listening to me."

Ophelia wrapped her hand around his wrist and squeezed. Startled, he pulled back, releasing Margaret.

"What the hell was that?" Alex rubbed his wrist.

"You were hurting Margaret." Ophelia curled her lip.

"What? Tesoro, are you okay?"

"I'm fine. But what happened? You're burning up," Margaret mumbled.

"It's all the energy. I feel like I'm gonna explode."

"Ready yourselves, we are walking out. Take in a breath—hold it," Zachary instructed.

"Maybe you should stop talking. It's going to make it harder," Ophelia pleaded.

The couple nodded.

Alex focused on his surroundings. Never had he seen so many spirits at one time. Well, not counting all his relatives that came to help him defeat Greta. But this was different. These are kids. It could easily be him or Margaret occupying a place at the Academy. The more dangerous the cases become, the harder it gets to protect her. She'll argue and say she doesn't need anyone looking out for her, but his world was one that defied the confines of the living.

They took a sharp left and turned into a small hallway. It was deserted.

His chest sawed, taking in life.

"Alex are you okay?" Margaret nuzzled next to him.

"My insides are on fire, but I'm managing. You?"

"I'm okay."

"This is the long stretch. Prepare," Zachary advised.

The gray walls of the Academy blurred into the dark sky. There was no sun. Alex fought to move without inhaling. The heat sizzling his flesh, making it more difficult to calm his struggle.

How much further, Alex mouthed.

"Soon, we are almost there. Concentrate." Zachary

quickened his pace.

Margaret clutched Alex's arm. "We're gonna make it." He nodded.

When the double doors to the gym were visible, Alex pushed ahead of Amry and Ophelia. Pulling Margaret, they blasted through and collapsed on the floor. Filling up their lungs and exhaling, they lay back on the cool oak. The room was free from outside heat due to the enormous stones used in its construction. Regaining their composure, they followed the celestials to the showers.

A drip from a rusty showerhead patted a small pool of water gathered around the drain, echoing through the barren walls. The cool, damp confinement of the stalls sizzled out the volcanic bubbles that had taken over Alex's highway to his organs.

"Is everyone well?" Zachary rippled, letting go of his solid form.

"Yeah. We're good." Margaret grinned.

"Babe, how's the burning?" Margaret directed her gaze toward Alex.

"Gone." Alex rubbed his temples.

"What the hell was that?"

"I think it was the concentration of all the electrical energy."

"Well that sucks. How you gonna be able to move around?"

"I'm not sure. Maybe if I clear my mind when we leave, I'll be better prepared to handle it. I wasn't expecting anything like that to happen, the grip was intense." Alex used the back of his hand to wipe off the sweat from his brow.

"Crap. I hope so." Margaret leaned in and kissed his lips."

"The room is down here." Ophelia pointed.

Alex and Margaret followed. By now, they had all

disbanded their corporal appearance. Like the tide coming in from the ocean, their celestial forms floated down the tunnel.

Alex grinned. It really was kind of cool.

Passing through the archway, he noticed an inscription etched in the stone above. He tugged Margaret's T-shirt and looked up. She immediately understood. Slipping her phone from her back pocket, she snapped a photo.

"We may not be able to phone home, but at least we can make a memory to take with us," she chuckled.

The teens abruptly stopped.

"Everybody knows something we don't. Why aren't we still moving?" Margaret asked.

"What is that?" Ophelia glided back, pointing to the cell phone in Margaret's hand.

"My phone. You haven't seen one before?" asked Margaret.
"

"In movies, we have seen some. But why did yours glow?" Ophelia stayed back.

"It has a camera in it. I took a picture. It wasn't a glow; it was a flash." Margaret held out the phone.

"Wait. You watch movies?"

"Yes. In the theater."

"Alex, this place is even weirder than we first thought."

"I guess it makes sense. If the Academy of Souls is sharing space with CTA Academy, if we have a theater, then so do they."

"But—they watch movies. They're dead. You get this, right?" Margaret said sarcastically.

Alex grinned.

"Let's get back to the phone," Sam insisted. "You can talk to people and then take pictures too? Far out."

"Didn't they have cell phones when you were living?"

"No." Sam put his hand out. Margaret laid it in his palm.

"Sam, when did you die?"

"1978, and Bethany in '79. We were meant to be together." Sam leaned in and kissed her cheek.

Alex and Margaret locked eyes and he smiled; he knew how Sam felt. Margaret was the love of his life, and if anything happened to her, he would ... "Okay, let's keep going. Explain to me again what exactly happened here."

Ophelia spilled out every detail of their encounter with Roger and Leon. Recounting the terror shook her being, pieces of color broke off, surrounding her celestial silhouette and illuminating the room.

Slowly, Alex stepped toward the scene of prior chaos. Allowing the energy to guide him, he ran his fingers lightly across the wall. Gasping, his throat tightened. Terror ripped through his flesh, peeling back layer by layer, reaching into his soul, filling it with paralyzing desperation. Quickly, he retracted his hand and stepped back.

"Alex. Are you all right?" Ophelia patted his back.

"I felt him. Roger. Everything he experienced when going through the gateway. He was terrified out of his mind."

Ophelia covered her face with her hands.

"It's not your fault. He chose his actions, not you. The gateway is still here."

"W-w-what?" Ophelia stammered.

"It's closed for now. But the portal is ready and waiting. This is the point of entry for *The Nowhere*. We won't find it anywhere else on campus. Unlike the in-between realms, this entry is very specific. I could feel the pull. That's probably why Roger brought Bethany here. If his twisted love plan didn't work, he knew he could only banish her soul from this specific place."

"Now what? Your *spidey sense* is going wild." Margaret observed.

Alex pulled down the sleeves of his hoodie to cover his arms. "I'm not sure. I think I'd need to have a better look at that book. Can Margaret and I stay in your room tonight?" he addressed Ophelia and Amry.

"Of course," Both girls sang out.

"We'll give you guys some privacy. Lia and I can bunk with Bethany for the night." Amry glanced at her friend.

"A sleepover—fun! Bethany grinned.

"We don't want to put you out. Alex and I can take the floor.

You girls can have your beds," Margaret replied.

"No. You take it. Besides, we don't sleep, remember? Only Lia needs her pleasant dreams, and she can crash on Bethany's bed."

"Absolutely," Bethany chimed in.

"Do not worry about us. You two need to get some rest," Ophelia persuaded.

"You convinced us." Alex rubbed his eyes. "I'm pretty worn out. How about you, *ciuccia mia?*"

Margaret lay her head on his shoulder. "I'm so ready for sleep."

"Ophelia, I do have one more question about your beginning, if you're up to it?" Alex asked softly.

Ophelia crossed her arms and dropped her chin. "Of course, what is your question?"

"You said that when Haven ran into the street, you were on the porch. Right?"

"Yes."

"Do you remember hearing anything?"

"I heard the rumbling of the car."

"What else?"

Ophelia's brows furrowed. "The birds. I heard the birds singing. But they stopped."

"When?"

"I don't understand."

"When did they stop?"

"I am not sure." Ophelia began rocking back and forth.

"Please, this is very important. "Alex was overanxious.

"Alex. Hold up a second." Margaret intervened.

"Ophelia it's okay. Sometimes it doesn't come right away. Give it time."

Alex weaved his fingers in Margaret's hand and nodded.

"They stopped when I ran into the street."

"I think that's it." Alex stood.

"Alex, can you elaborate for us?" Zachary asked.

"Why Ophelia is connected to the living. She wasn't supposed to die. Her life-force is tethered because it wasn't supposed to be here."

"But how do you know this?" Ophelia trembled.

"Because of the birds. My grandfather told me that when a soul is being released, the birds sing. But you said they stopped.

You weren't supposed to run out after Haven. In that moment, they knew there would be a disruption in the balance between the two worlds."

"What do we do? I mean it is too late to change what happened. Do I stay like this forever?" Ophelia muttered.

"I don't know. Let's get back to the room and maybe I can find something in the book."

AFTER REPEATING the excruciating journey back to the girl's dorm room, Alex and Margaret collapsed on Amry's bed. It was closest to the window and Margaret liked having the view.

"Alex, I need to say something. Back there, with Ophelia ..."

"I came on too strong. I know that's why you interjected."

"She's frightened of who she is. You out of all of us

understand what that's like. You need to work on your people, and ghost skills."

"I know, I'll try to be more aware." Alex sat up.

"You better." Margaret ran her fingers down his back. "There's something else."

"What else did I do?"

"It's not so much what you do, it's what you don't do."

"I'm not following."

Margaret cleared her throat. "When you're in the middle of a case and something is dangerous, you seem to always treat the women around you like we're fragile. You tend to rely on the guys. But this is a direct contradiction to what you've said about me. I hear tough, spunky, capable, but sometimes you don't back up the words."

"I just don't want you or any other girl to get hurt."

"I love that you love me, but remember, we protect each other. Women are not little China dolls that are gonna break when it gets rough. For Christ's sake, look at your mom and grandma. I don't know anyone, man, or woman, more capable than they are. It's like me coming here with you. I know you were pissed but you never even gave me the opportunity to decide for myself. You made that decision on your own. Not fair."

The words stung him. It never even entered his mind that he'd been basically taken her—women for granted. Assuming they needed to be rescued. Alex tried to suppress the rising wave of nausea. He'd been doing the same thing that had been done to him most of his life...assuming. People assumed they knew everything about him based on the hand he was dealt. But they knew very little. To think he was responsible for the same act of ignorance repulsed him.

"Tesoro, I'm so very sorry. There are no words, no excuses."

"Change. Just change."

Alex lay his head on her shoulder, and she pulled him close.

"Can you help with this?" Alex pleaded.

"Your binder?"

"Yeah."

"Sure. Arms up."

Margaret pulled up Alex's T-shirt and threw it on Ophelia's bed. With a firm grip on either side, she shimmied up the binder over his chest, and then yanked it past his head.

"How's that?"

"So much better. But I'm really itchy."

"Turn around."

Alex scooted around with his back facing her. Margaret lightly pressed her nails across the middle of his back, sawing across and then up and down. The edges of his second skin had left an imprint circling his torso.

"Is that thing getting tight?" she asked concerned.

"A little. It's the same one from two years ago. So is my spare," Alex sighed.

"You need to get some new ones when we get back. You're all marked up."

"I need to get surgery when we get back. I can't take much more of this."

"I know. Have you decided not to wait?"

"Yeah. I really wanted a car first, but this is really getting to me."

"Car, shmar. You got me. Your personal, full-time chauffeur. And you know how much I love to drive."

"I do." Alex smirked.

"Seriously. Get your surgery. The car can wait a little longer. If you're this uncomfortable, I think it should be taken care of."

Alex nodded. He loved her so much. She always understood.

She got him.

"Better?"

He slipped his T-shirt back on.

"Yes, thanks. Now, let's have a look at this book."

"I got a question. I wanted to ask earlier, but with everything Ophelia's had to deal with, I didn't want to add to the weirdness. Have you noticed she smells sweet? Like flowers or something."

Margaret furrowed her brow.

"I did. But like you said, too much already going on."

The couple hunkered down under the blanket, and Alex held the book up for both to see.

"Look at this." Alex pointed to a drawing.

"It sort of looks like Dante's Inferno." Margaret bit her bottom lip.

"It's a rendition of the in-between realm, the Underworld. This is where Zachary was for over five hundred years."

"That poor guy. How he's still sane is incredible." Margaret pulled the covers up.

"I think being half dark sorcerer is probably why. Another soul would've gone looney already. There's a reason they're hunting him. I don't think he knows how badass he is."

"I think you're right. He's like a lamb in the woods. But I got a feeling if provoked, the lamb will quickly turn into the wolf."

Alex turned the page. Horrified, he sat up.

"This is bad. This is very bad." He tapped his forehead to the book.

"What is it?"

"I was right about the location of *The Nowhere*. Only ten gateways exist around the entire world. One of them is here, another in the in-between realm of Purgatory. The rest are scattered among the living world. Anyway, it states that the realm can be opened in two ways. One by a sorcerer and the other ... I don't like this."

"What?"

"The other way is, if two souls of magick descent simultaneously repeat the spell, then it will access the passageway. And, this is the part I really hate. The person who initiated it, can do it again without the other soul. It's like they hold a permanent key to the lock. This means there's a chance Roger can find his way back."

"Oh brother. This is getting exasperating. We have Ophelia looking for Haven, who's being held by a loony Soul Gatherer. Zachary, who's being hunted by a squad of evil whatevers, and Leon, who is pissed off because he blames the dead teen squad for his best friends' ticket to the abyss. Now, we get to throw in Roger. A crazy, maniacal ghost, with a mad crush on Bethany, and may find a way to crawl out of *The Nowhere,* and into our backyard. Did I leave anything out?"

"Well, there is the thing about staying too long. But not to worry, I got it covered."

Margaret turned onto her side and rested her head on the palm of her hand.

"Explain."

"Remember that conversation I had with Gram? She told me not to come because it's dangerous."

"Yes, not that it meant anything to you. Deaf ears and all."

"Yeah, I get it. Anyway, the reason it's so dangerous is because if a living soul stays too long in a realm for the dead, they can't go home."

"Huh. This would have been nice to know before I latched onto your hoodie."

"Would it have changed things for you?"

Margaret paused. "Not in the least."

"I rest my case."

"So how are you keeping track?"

Alex slipped his phone out of the back pocket of his jeans. Swiping it, he held it up for Margaret to see the screen. Numbers scrolled in a countdown.

"When this is done, so are we."

"Jeez. We only have thirty-six hours to get this done?"

"Yup."

"What happens if your battery runs out of juice? We won't have a clue about how much time is left." Margaret questioned.

"Weird thing is, since we've gotten here, my battery has stayed fully charged. I think the electrical current is affecting the phone's battery. Check yours."

Margaret slipped her phone from her pocket and nodded.

"Mines at full charge too. But we should get back out there. Why are we wasting time sleeping?"

"Because if we don't get some rest, we'll be too drained to do anything. Have you noticed your body feels weighted?"

"I did. I thought it was just because I've been on petrified alert since our journey to the gym."

"No. It's the energy here. You can smell the sulfur in the air. They're pulling at our life force. We need to slow down our metabolism and sleep for a while. Besides, Mr. Johnson won't be here until tomorrow. I really need to see what he's found out, if anything at all. I sure hope he has."

Margaret lay her head down and scooted closer to Alex. He gently brushed back her bangs with his fingertips and kissed her forehead. Snuggling close, they let sleep guide them into their dreams.

THE UNDERWORLD

"Haven! Watch out!"

"Wake up." Margaret shook Alex.

"What happened?"

"You were having a nightmare. You shouted out Haven's name a few times."

Alex sat up and drew his knees to his chest.

"She's running out of time. I understand now. It's the same for her as it is us. Too long in an in-between realm, and you never leave."

"But what about the Soul Gatherer? And Zachary? He was in the underworld for over five hundred years. And you heard Ophelia, this soul guy has been around for a very long time. They both managed to leave the in-between realms."

"You're forgetting one thing."

"What?"

"They're both sorcerers."

"You think the Soul Gatherer is a sorcerer, too?"

"I do."

"What proof do you have?"

"None. But this is what my *know* is telling me. I felt it in the dream."

"All righty then."

"I'm gonna get in the shower. Care to join me?" Alex curled his bottom lip.

"Hmm. Tempting. But since we're currently in the land of, *walls don't mean a thing*, I'll go after you."

"I'll miss you."

"I'm sure you can weather through without me."

"Yes. But I won't like it." He smiled broadly.

Shutting the bathroom door, Alex brushed his hand across the frame. He wondered how many souls had passed through this very spot before him. Closing his eyes, he let his body free itself from the confines of the living. Letting go of the tether that protected him from the spirit world. Opening the door and pushing out the clutter, he let them in—all of them. Teens from everywhere flooded his mind. Flashes of conversation, moments forever captured in the walls of the room. Centuries of souls, happy, sad, eager, hesitant, hopeful, hopeless, they all resided here at one time or another. A wave of nausea rumbled through his stomach.

Slowly pulling away, the connection broke. He hadn't noticed when they started, but tears stained his cheeks, stinging their way into his pores. Alex turned the knob in the shower and a stream of tepid water sprayed the stall floor. He stepped in and lowered his head under the cleansing liquid cascading down his back. Too many. He let too many souls in at once. Their essence drained him, like drops of blood dripping into in an unseen pipeline to feed the energy of the Academy.

Standing with both hands on the shower wall, he took three deep breaths and exhaled. He couldn't tell Margaret. She'd be pissed at him for doing something so foolish. He knew what could happen if he lowered his defenses, but he wanted to make a connection. He wouldn't have this chance again. Once they returned to the living, the Academy of Souls would become a memory. He yearned to absorb as much as he could.

Too much anesthetizing and he might not be able to understand those who need him. Keeping emotions in check was one thing, turning them off was not a luxury he could abide by.

"Hey, you almost done it there. It's my turn." Margaret called.

"Yeah. Come on in. I'm just finishing up."

Margaret brushed against him. Peeling off her jeans and hoodie, she stepped into the now steaming, hot liquid.

"Thanks for leaving the shower on for me. It's toasty."

"For you, anything."

"Yeah, yeah. I see the bullshit is knee deep this morning."

"Not one bit. I would do anything for you."

"Alex? Margaret?" Ophelia sang out.

"We're in here. I'll be out in a sec."

Alex gingerly pulled on his boxers and slipped the dreaded binder over his head, shimmying and tugging it in place. Jeans and a hoodie, and he was ready.

"I hate that we have to put on the same clothes."

Margaret pulled back the curtain.

"Me too. But at least we're clean."

"I know. I'm going out there to talk to Ophelia."

"Okay. I'll be ready in a few minutes."

Alex puckered his lips and blew a kiss across the molecules. Grabbing his socks, he partially opened the door, trying not to let the cold air in, he quickly exited.

"Mr. Johnson is here. Amry is bringing him up."

"Good. I had another dream last night."

"About Haven? Was she all right?"

"Right now, yes. But I don't think for long. We need to get to her."

"Alex, I've been trying for 108 years. Every time I think I am getting close; it turns out to be nothing. I do think she's in an in-between realm, I believe that with all my heart. But there are twenty-eight that we know of. What about the ones we don't know about? And if he keeps moving her, how are we ever going to find her?"

"Slow down. Let's see what Johnson has to say. He might have found the solution already."

"I hope so."

The bathroom door flung open, and Margaret stepped out, towel drying her hair.

"There's something I was thinking about in the shower. If the two souls must be of magick descent, then does that mean Roger and Leon are sorcerers?" asked Margaret.

"No. But somewhere in their bloodlines, there had to be at least one in each. I guess they figured it out." Alex glanced out the window.

"Whew. The thought of those two idiots having any kind of powers really riled me."

"Not to worry. I'm pretty sure they're just average dead teens."

"Comforting." Margaret smirked.

Rap, Rap. The door shook slightly.

"Lia, let us in." Amry requested.

Ophelia turned the knob and pulled the door slightly ajar. There were multiple souls floating through the hallway. Amry stood in front of the open crack shielding the view to the room. She slipped through, followed by Mr. Johnson, and the rest of the crew.

"Mr. Johnson, this is Alex ..."

"McKenna." Johnson extended his hand.

"You know who I am?" Alex shook his hand.

"You're the only male breather in the room. Who else would you be?"

"Good point."

"If everyone doesn't mind the floor, there's more space." Amry waved her arm.

Bethany and Sam clustered together, Zachary and Amry sat next to Ophelia, Alex scooted closer to Margaret, and Mr. Johnson found his place in the center of all of them.

"I know you're all waiting for news, and I do have some information. But not as much as I thought I would. Ophelia, I did find out where the Soul Gatherer has been slipping off to. I'm not sure if that's where he has Haven, though. There were reports of a little girl resembling the description Amry gave me, but nothing solid. My sources from the in-between realms tell me he is in a very dangerous in-between—the Underworld. I do know a little about this place, but only enough to tell you to be very careful. If you plan on going through the gateway, be prepared. This is an extremely dark place."

Zachary stood.

"I know all too well how treacherous the Underworld realm is."

"What do you mean?" Johnson asked.

"Zachary spent five hundred years there." Alex replied.

"Son, how did you make it out with your faculties? Five hundred years is a long time for any in-between realm, but the Underworld is treacherous."

Zachary ignored the question.

"Maybe we discuss this at another time. Right now, our focus is on Haven," said Alex.

Mr. Johnson went on with his news.

"In addition, they've told me that Haven can't stay in the realms much longer. She's dangerously close to becoming a permanent being. A soul that forgets who they are, and where they came from. They're destined to never take the light and inhabit the in-between world for eternity. Which is why young man, you will give me an explanation when this is all over."

Zachary narrowed his eyes and then looked away.

"I guess the answer is, I have to go to the Underworld in-between." Alex stated.

"No!" Zachary shouted.

"Zachary, I can't even imagine what it was like for you. But if we're gonna save Haven, then I have to go."

"Wait. What's this *I* bullshit?" Margaret snapped.

"You're not going on this one. I can't help Haven and worry about you at the same time."

"Have you forgotten our talk last night so quickly? When the hell has it been up to you to say what I can and cannot do? Listen Alex, you don't get to make decisions for me. I'm going with you."

"No, but."

"Me too. She is my sister," Ophelia chimed.

"I'm not letting Lia go without me. I'm going too." Amry stood.

"You guys came to save me when Roger was going to throw me into *The Nowhere*. I can't let you do this on your own. I'm in," Bethany said firmly.

"Well, I guess the gangs all here. Can't let your screw-ups go without a little muscle." Sam smirked.

All of them stood and joined Amry.

"We're going. End of story, McKenna," Amry said.

Alex lowered his head; he knew they were right. It wasn't his place telling any of them what they can and can't do. Raising his head, he caught Margaret's gaze and smirked. "Okay. We all go. Zachary, you too?"

"Yes," Zachary mumbled.

"What? Why?" Ophelia asked.

"Because I am the only one who has been there before. I

know that place better than anyone. If I am with you, you have an ample chance of finding Haven, and finding her quicker."

"Mr. Johnson, will you open the portal to the Underworld for us? The book states it must be a sorcerer." Amry asked.

"Oh child, I think you misunderstand. I'm not a sorcerer. Just an old soul who won't give up on my mission."

"What mission is that?"

"To help as many of the lost as I can."

"Why?" Amry leaned in.

Mr. Johnson cleared his throat and then glanced out the window. Looking down at his shoes, he spoke softly.

"My daughter, Elizabeth Grace. She was taken many years ago by a demonic celestial. I tried to get to her before it whisked her away, but I was too late. For years I hunted for her, but when I found my precious daughter, she was lost. Elizabeth had been in the Purgatory in-between for too long. She had no idea who I was. Worse, she had become a permanent being. No thoughts of life, her mother, where she came from. Delirium replaced the sweet girl I once knew. I vowed that day to never stop. I will not take the light as long as there are lost souls like your sister, and my Elizabeth Grace."

"We don't need anyone else; we have Zachary." Alex's eyes narrowed.

Mr. Johnson stood.

"You are a sorcerer young man?"

"He's half sorcerer. Dark magick," Alex replied.

"That's why you survived all those years. This is good." Johnson grinned.

"Good? How?" Ophelia's eyes widened.

"He will be immune to the darkness that consumes the Underworld. Not only can he guide you, but he can protect you."

"I do not know how to use the darkness inside me. And I do not know how to open the portal." Zachary gulped.

"We have the book. Margaret, can you look for the incantation?" Alex asked.

"Sure."

Margaret leafed through the pages, perusing through the words quickly.

"Got it!"

"I told you I will go, but I do not have the skill to perform the task." Zachary stated.

"I'll say the words with you." Alex smiled. "I'm not a sorcerer but I do have some abilities of my own. Maybe they'll help. Zachary, believe in yourself. Know that you can do this, reach deep into yourself and let it free. It's your own pessimism that binds you. You can do this, I know you can." Alex turned to the old man. "Mr. Johnson, you're our witness. If we don't return in a few days, please tell Headmaster Abernathy. I think it's also a good time for you to leave. You wouldn't want to be an unwilling ticket holder of a trip to the Underworld." Alex furrowed his brow.

Johnson nodded and hastily exited the room.

"Everybody ready for this?" Alex requested.

"Trust me. None of you are ready for this." Zachary warned.

"Unlike *The Nowhere*, a doorway to an in-between can be opened from virtually anywhere. We should all get to one side and use the other end of the room for the gateway. Can I have the spell, Tesoro?"

Margaret handed Alex the book. "Okay Zachary, we read together."

Alex closed the gap between them. Holding the book up for both to see, he nodded.

"Everyone stay close. Hold on to each other, and when I say jump, you go. Zachary—believe."

Amry and Ophelia tightly interlocked their fingers,

Bethany had Sam's arm in a death grip, and Margaret hooked her finger around one of Alex's belt loops.

The boys recited the spell in unison.

"I summon the passage to the world like no other. Not the top, not the middle, but deep down under. Open the gate, seal my fate. Show me the Underworld, guide my way. With my light I shall pay."

"Again!" Alex shouted.

The boys repeated the spell until the ground beneath their feet rumbled, forcing the wood slats to shake from the seismic vibrations. Wobbling back and forth, they struggled to keep their balance. A thunderous clap struck its way into Alex's head. He shrieked with pain and released the book. Scrambling he dropped to the floor and scooped it up. Pressing it tightly to his chest he winced when the crackle came again. Like the sound of a leather whip, *crack, crack,* it rang through the room with venomous intensity.

Ophelia screamed as the far wall ripped apart, catapulting pieces of stone across the room.

A shard of rock nicked Alex's cheek and a small river of blood trickled down to his lips, coating them with the acid taste of metal. He skipped a breath as the center of the wall collapsed inward, revealing a spinning shaft of blue and purple light.

"This is it!" Alex yelled, "Margaret, don't let go."

"Never!"

Leaping into the spinning prisms of violet and sapphire, Alex struggled. His shallow breath robbed his brain of oxygen, and his head drooped to his chest. With each exaggerated blink, his eyelids grew heavier until he lost consciousness.

WATCH OUT FOR THE HAIRY KAPPA

"Hey. Wake up. We're here," said Margaret The rapid tapping on his cheek stung. "What happened?"

"You passed out. Well, we passed out. I just woke up quicker thanks to Ophelia."

"I tried to get you too, but I couldn't. I saw you both collapsing as we were going through. Sorry, Alex. You were just out of my reach."

"No. I'm glad you were able to get Margaret first, thank you."

"This is freaking me out, would you look at this place!" Sam exclaimed.

The Underworld lived up to its reputation. Grey, murky water flowed through a river that separated the realm into two different but equally dismal patches of land. Canopied by a sky of dense, ominous clouds, their gaseous bodies plump with the stench of rotten eggs. To think the rainwater to be clear and fresh, would be naïve.

The left plain was everything you'd imagine hell to be. Fire burned throughout the terrain, while bolts of lightning repeatedly lit up the welkin and sliced its way through blackened trees. Cloudy puddles of water were plopped down, randomly covering the surface like tiny pools of poison.

The right plain held its own glory of a Satan like kingdom. Where fire prevailed on the left plain, the right embraced a thick oil like substance. Dripping from the branches of dead and shriveled trees, it blanketed the ground with gooey tar pits. Pockets of solid earth were sparse and placed amid the black goop in a diamond shaped pattern. Scattered like pieces to a puzzle, it made hiking through the right plain nearly impossible. Screams of agonized pain howled in the distance.

Zachary tightened his fists.

"Where did you stay for all those years?" Alex inquired.

"I kept mostly to the land on the left. There are caves, and makeshift stone shelters that other creatures constructed. It shields from lightning and fires. I did venture across the right plain, but the hot tar makes navigating the land extremely treacherous. And there is not much shelter, only a source of unending torture, if you're unlucky enough to get trapped by a hairy Kappa."

"What the hell is a *hairy kappa*?" Alex raised a brow.

"It is reminiscent of an ogre who is eternally hungry—for the pleasures of pain. Once they trap you, your chances of escape are not very good. They are cunning and strong. I did meet a spirit once who was fortunate enough to get away, but he was half mad by the time we crossed paths."

"What do they look like?"

"They stand tall—six feet in stature, furry like an ape, with a weave of hair that resembles a bowl positioned on the top of their head, it is eternally filled with water."

"Did you say a bowl of water?"

"Indeed. You must be especially careful around a body of water. They can make it appear clear, cool, and inviting. When you bend down to take a sip, they pull you in and drag you to their lair. That is where they hold all their victims until they go completely insane. Once that happens, they manipulate what is left of the poor bastard's life force into an energy ball, which they use to keep the oil pits bubbling."

"What happens to the spirit?"

"It is obliterated. As if they never existed."

"Wait. You said watch out for water. I don't see any water, just oily gunk."

"Beyond the oil, further into the plain, there are pools of murky water just like you see over there." Zachary pointed to the left side of the land. "The Kappa create the illusion of salvation in the middle of all this—*death*. The pools appear azure blue, and so clear, you can see white rock nestled at the bottom. Too many souls have been prey to them while I spent my years here. I was almost one of them. But a girl rescued me right before I was doomed in its clutches. Ruby. She was kind, and definitely did not belong here."

"What happened to her?" Alex clenched Margaret's hand. "She was banished by a powerful wizard for rejecting him. I tried to bring her with us when my uncle rescued me, but in our last moments together, a Kappa tracked us. She sacrificed herself so that I could be saved." Zachary turned away.

"And what about the left plain? Any creatures of hell we need to watch out for?"

"There is no safe destination in the Underworld, just the lesser of the evils. The creatures that exist in the left plain can be equally terrifying, but they are easier to avoid. Unlike the Kappa, they are small and slower, we can easily outrun anyone of them.

The trick is to not let your guard down. If they cannot get close, they cannot do damage. I realize this is not offering any comfort, but it is all we have. Honestly, if this Soul Gatherer exists here, and he has Haven and others with him, he must be powerful. Protecting himself and the others he has taken would not be easy."

"I've been worried about that. I know he's rumored to be a lonely man who takes souls for company, but I felt all along he had to be a sorcerer, and a skilled one. To avert detection for all this time, there has to be magick involved." Alex exhaled. "Left plain?"

"The lesser of the two evils," said Zachary.

"Everybody okay?" Alex asked.

Everyone nodded.

"Please, follow me and do everything I ask you to. The lightning strikes the ground every ten minutes. We will seek shelter and wait it out when it does. It only lasts for twenty seconds, then it returns to the sky. Stay away from the river and any other body of water we come to. There is a patch of desolate, but clear land about five miles that way." Zachary pointed East.

"That is where we will try first. If the Soul Gatherer is a sorcerer, he could offer protection anywhere. But I think he will likely choose a spot that is easier and takes less energy to secure."

"That makes sense. I'm going to try and connect with Haven. If I can, maybe we can get a confirmation of where she is. It doesn't always work; I could use your energy to make me stronger." Alex said.

"Stronger? How can you do that?" Ophelia questioned.

"He has a few tricks up his sleeve." Margaret smirked.

"I can call her with my thoughts. The stronger I am, the more powerful the connection. With all your energy, it's a boost to my own abilities."

"He can also move things with his mind. But that's only when he's sleeping. I'm waiting for that one to materialize when he's awake. It's gonna be so cool." Margaret grinned.

"Ciucciamia," Alex sighed.

"What? Just proud of my guy."

"If the love fest is over, can we go find Ophelia's sister?" Sam balked.

"The lightning is about to start up. We must get to our first shelter before it hits the ground. You can try to connect with Haven there." Zachary looked at the sky.

The fires raged in a pattern of roadblocks, reaching out with their tentacles to incinerate, while murky puddles bubbled, waiting to swallow the careless soul.

The group stayed close together, following Zachary's moves. He led them to a rock formation that offered a ceiling of shelter to shield them from the upcoming electric show. Alex closed his eyes and envisioned Haven.

"Can everyone get close to me, please?"

The celestials crowded around him while Margaret took a step back. Each one placed their hand on Alex's shoulder, arm or back. His body jolted like a switch had been flipped. Their energy surged, carrying the charge he needed to send his thoughts out to Haven.

"I see a child. Long brown hair, she's wearing a green dress. She's not facing me so I can't be sure it's Haven. Wait. She has

flowers peeking out of a side pocket. I think it's ... rose petals?"

"That is her. Haven," Ophelia said firmly.

"How can you be so sure?" Alex asked.

"She was picking them the day of our beginning. Before the accident. I scolded her, told her our mother would be upset because she was so proud of her roses. It was stupid. They were just petals from one flower."

"Wait. Lia, I bet that's why you always smell like flowers. I couldn't get the scent until now, but it's roses." Amry smiled.

"That's part of your connection to the living, and to Haven. The garden sent the aroma of life with you in your beginning." Alex beamed.

Alex raised his hand in a stop motion. The figure of a little girl appeared like a projection onto a screen."

"Alex, how the hell are you doing that?"

"I'm not sure. I think it's because their energy is boosting my *know* to a level it's never been before. It's cool, though. I just knew what to do."

"This is beyond cool." Margaret's eyes widened.

"I can't see who it is, but someone's talking to her. She's shaking her head, agreeing with them. Or maybe acknowledging. I'm not sure. I don't want to call her until I'm sure it's safe. It could be the Soul Gatherer." Alex squinted.

"Let us concentrate on the where. What does everyone see? It might help me determine the location," Zachary commented.

"The walls are layered with slats of wood," whispered Amry.

"There is a window to the left. I see gushing water. It's black," Ophelia said anxiously.

"I see it!" Amry exclaimed.

"We do to," Bethany and Sam replied.

"Zachary, do you know where the black waterfall is?" Alex asked.

"There are two actually, and this presents a problem. They are on opposite sides of the plain. We need something else. There. That is what I was looking for." Zachary pointed.

"What is it?" Alex stretched his neck.

"The water has violet crystals running through it. That is the Purple Fountain. It is the only body of water that contains color. There is a core of Amethyst in the mountain. The rushing water slowly chips it away. It makes the falls have a purple sparkle. I know how to get to Haven." Zachary grinned.

"The lightning eased up," said Sam.

Using his boosted abilities, Alex tried calling to the little girl using his thoughts. The child stiffened and slowly turned her head over her right shoulder. He raised his finger to his lips and she gently nodded. *We're coming Haven.*

The connection was broken the minute everyone disbursed, but the pain wasn't. Alex wiped the beads of sweat off his forehead. The little girl was scared. That didn't fit the picture of a lonely old man looking for company. His proclivity for children just added to the strangeness. *Why not the company of other adults to engage in conversation? Surely if he's that lonely, he would rather fill his time with celestials that could give him companionship.* The reasons disturbed him, but he wasn't sure if his suspicions were right. There was no need to add to the mounting anxiety Ophelia had already gone through all these years.

THE GROUND OFFERED no help in their journey to get to Haven quickly. The fires merciless heat forced them to take a less direct route. And the water, no reprieve. Too murky and thick, one step in the wrong direction and you could find yourself drowning in a pool equivalent to quicksand and oil. Slow and steady, they followed Zachary further into the plain and away from the portal home. Lightning burst across the black clouds, crackling with loud booms and illuminating the already ominous sky. Alex counted down ten minutes in his head.

"Zachary, it's almost time for the ground show."

"I am aware. There is a small cave just around the bend. It will be tight, but we will all fit."

The road veered off to the left, butting up to a large base of the grayest mountain Alex had ever seen. No trees, or signs of plant life. Stretching his fingers, he ran them along the wall. The color would suggest the rock was cool to the touch—it was on fire. He quickly retracted and blew on his fingertips.

The cave was about twenty feet into the bend, and Zachary was right, it definitely was cramped. They piled in, any way they could. Being literally on top of each other was much better than getting struck by lightning.

"Everyone in?" Zachary asked.

"I think we're all good," Alex spoke, "Zachary, were you ever struck by lightning when you were here?"

"I was. It was beyond frightening."

"What happens? I mean, I know if Margaret or I were to get hit, it's a pretty good bet we're dead. But without stating the obvious, what could possibly happen to you guys?"

"It is similar to when a light bulb glows with a surge of electricity and blows out. If we short out, it has the same effect. All our energy is gone. Presumably, we die for good. No existence of any kind after that. I was lucky, it barely caught me. The pain was indescribable, and it took me time to recover, but as I indicated, I was fortunate."

"Should we try calling out to Haven again?" Ophelia asked.

"No. She knows we're coming. I don't want to risk tipping off the gatherer," Alex stated.

"He is correct, Ophelia. Better to have the element of surprise in our favor. It is safe, the lightning stopped," said Zachary.

A light wind carried the heat from the fire, stacking it like a brick wall. It was the intensity of your worst Summer day with no cool drink. Sweat beaded up along Alex's forehead and upper lip. Trickling down his cheeks and jaw, a few droplets rested on his mouth, stinging his lips. The salty taste brought nausea to the ripples of acid in his stomach. Pushing their way up into the back of his throat, the sour taste was forced back by a coughing fit.

"You okay?" Margaret whispered.

"Yup. Just my usual damn stomach talking to me."

"Follow me ... We need to get to the cover of that group of trees over there," Zachary shouted.

It was like a mirage in the middle of the desert. About fifty feet directly in front of them was a dense grove of topiary wonder.

"How are they here in the middle of all this?" Alex wondered.

"It is a trap of sorts. However, I believe you and Margaret will not be affected."

"What do you mean, a trap?"

"It is used to snare spirits by luring them in with their beauty among all the desolation. Once you are there, it has a hypnotic effect. You remain while the trees slowly drain you, that is what keeps them green. I was stuck once. Ruby pulled me out. Twice she saved me, and I repaid her by leaving her in the clutches of a Kappa."

"Why do you think Margaret and I will be immune?"

"Your life force runs on a different frequency than a celestial. Correct?"

"Yes. Oh, wait. I get it. You think the trees won't recognize our frequency and won't be able to tap into it."

"Precisely."

"Well—let's hope you're right."

The cracking of a whip followed by a loud boom indicated they had run out of time. Lightning had hit the ground about ten yards away. Running at full speed, Alex and Margaret darted to avoid the bolts of death. Without leaving their side, the rest of the friends floated beside them.

"Go! Get yourselves to the trees," Alex shouted.

"No. We are not leaving without you. We stay together," Zachary argued.

"If the whole lot of us gets hit, Haven doesn't stand a chance. Go!"

But none of them paid any attention to Alex's warning.

Insisting on staying in a group, they reached the grove together.

"You're the most stubborn bunch of dead people I've ever met," Alex barked.

"Us? Look who is breathing in the middle of the Underworld. Do not snap at us about following directions. You would not have listened if we told you two not to come. I believe we are at an impasse." Zachary smirked.

"Point taken," Alex muttered.

"Are you sure these trees were a good idea for protection? I mean, lightning can strike trees down," said Margaret.

"Not these trees. They are protected. It is all part of this foul world," Zachary replied.

Alex and Margaret slid down the side of a trunk and rested. "The flames are kind of beautiful. They remind me of that painting we saw at the fair in Hicksville, remember? The entire painting was black and white, except for one red balloon a little girl was holding. The red and orange of the flames resemble that same look. They're beautiful against the gray and black of this world. Like a beacon of light," Margaret sighed.

"Careful. They're fooling you."

Alex narrowed his eyes. "What do you mean?"

"I can feel their pull. They want to draw us in. Capture our life with the fire. None of the spirits can be harmed by the flames, I think they're here for living souls that may get trapped or banished. If you let yourself go, it will be like a moth drawn to a flame. You wouldn't be able to stop. So please stop staring," Alex pleaded.

"Whoa. You're right. As soon as I broke the connection by turning away, I felt it. Like a cord was cut. So damn weird. Hey, check out our group of merry ghosts."

Alex gazed up at the five hovering celestials. With wide eyes, their gaze was frozen. He turned to see what they were fixated on. In the center of the bluff stood a large, stoic, Weeping Willow.

"Did you see that tree when we first got here?" Alex asked.

"Uh. Nope." Margaret shook her head.

"Me neither."

"So what? It just appeared out of nowhere?" Margaret stood.

"I don't think so. Look. See those other trees circling the outer edges? I think when we first got here, they were covering it."

"They moved?" Margaret's jaw dropped.

"Yup. Pretty sure. They were much denser. I swear."

"Well that's not creepy at all. I think we've got a bigger problem. None of these guys seem to be able to function. They're all just floating like a puff of smoke. I mean they're expressions are completely void of coherence. Hey. *Ophelia. Amry.* See, nothing."

Alex got up and waved his hand in front of Zachary. The teen remained focused on the Willow.

"This is what he was telling me about. And he was right. You and I are immune. We need to snap them out of it before we miss the next interval of lightening reprieve."

Margaret tried shaking Amry, but her hands passed through the teens body, scattering molecules of color in the air before settling down to re-formulate her billowing spirit.

"I guess that was pretty stupid," Margaret sighed.

Alex grinned.

"Kind of. But I have another idea. Let's float them to the edge, away from the Willow."

"How? We can't get a hold of them."

"Push them. The force of the air should carry them away. They'll break up but reassemble like Amry just did. It'll take a few shoves, but I think it'll work."

"I love you McKenna, but this is ridiculous."

"Do you have any other suggestions?"

"I guess not. This sort of reminds me of *The Wizard of Oz*. You know, when Dorothy falls asleep in the field of poppies. What did they use to wake her up? I can't remember."

"Snow. But that's not gonna help us. You ready?"

"Yup."

"I'll start with Zachary, and then Sam and Bethany. You get Ophelia and Amry," said Alex.

Margaret nodded.

Alex made a fist and pulled back his arm. Then, like taking a pitch on the mound he let it go. Zachary's spirit broke apart like hundreds of colorful Lego pieces. When they connected again, he was about five feet away.

"It worked. Hurry, let's keep going."

Margaret took aim at Ophelia and let it go. Her fist shattered the teen into beautiful little specks of bursting color. Just like Zachary, she came together a few feet away.

"Hey, it helps if you blow out air right after you swat. I got Zachary much further away the second time." Alex puckered.

"Okay."

Once Alex had Zachary at the edge of the grove, it only took a few seconds for him to be released from the tree's hypnotic clutches.

"Zachary. Help us. We've only got about a minute before the next interval."

Zachary quickly teleported back to Amry, Sam and Bethany. Wrapping his arms around them in a bear hug, he brought them to safety.

"What the hell happened?" Sam raised a brow.

"I'll explain later. But now, we need to go. The lightning's returned to the sky." Alex stated.

Trying to make the most of their ten-minute ground time, the teens hustled as quickly as they could. But having two breathers with them meant not being able to use their ghostly attributes to get around.

"We're slowing you down." Alex shook his head.

"Nonsense. We are not that far away. Maybe another three or four of these stops and we should be there," Zachary reassured him.

"Bethany! Beth!" Sam yelled.

Alex and Zachary turned around. Sam was furiously scrambling around the area.

"Sam, what's wrong? Where's Bethany?"

"I don't know. She was right here. I was distracted by that last jolt of lightning, and when I turned back, she was gone. This is crazy. She wouldn't just leave. Something's wrong."

Alex shivered. He held up both arms—gooseflesh.

"Hey, your arms are loaded." Margaret frowned.

"Yeah. Whatever's going on, it's got my *spidey sense* at attention. We need to find Bethany."

"We got less than ten minutes until the next strike. Why don't we split up? The mountain is East, so we can rule that out.

Zachary and Sam, you go North. Margaret and I will take South, and Ophelia and Amry go West. Zachary, where's the next shelter?"

"Approximately a mile North. I constructed a sufficient shelter years ago."

"Okay. Everyone meets there as soon as you can. Don't get stuck out here. Any longer than five or six minutes and head for safety," Alex instructed.

Alex took a firm grip on Margaret's hand. He didn't want any surprises like Sam was dealing with. They traced their steps back from the direction they had just come. The space was wide open— nothing to shield someone from sight.

"She's not here. Clearly, we can see the entire terrain.

Other than going back to the grove, I think we need to follow a different direction," Margaret suggested.

"We both know she didn't just wander off. She'd never leave Sam's side willingly. Let's search around a little more. Maybe what we're looking for isn't in plain sight."

"What do you mean?"

"We're in a realm of spirits and magick. Just because we can't see something, doesn't mean it's not here. We shouldn't take anything at face value."

"Huh. Makes sense. What should we look for?"

"I'm not sure. But I got a feeling we'll know if we see it."

"Like that?" Margaret tilted her head.

Alex set his gaze in the direction she pointed. In the middle of one of the many pools of watery muck, there stood three brown, leafy bushes.

"Okay. That's odd. I don't remember seeing that before, and I'm pretty sure it would have stuck out."

"Me neither. What now? Got any tricks up those sleeves?"

"Actually, I do. It's that spell Gram taught me to help reveal ghosts who were hiding. Remember? It's from the case we did last Spring. The little boy who was confused. He didn't realize he was dead, and he did some fierce poltergeist crap to his parents. The spell enabled me to see him so we could communicate."

"I do remember. You guided him to cross over."

"I'll try it on those bushes. If there's more there, the spell will reveal the true picture."

Alex inched closer. He removed a small satchel from his front pocket. Loosening the cord, he removed a white cloth containing a single crystal and clutched it in his left hand. Cinching the bag, he returned it to his pocket.

"When the hell did you start carrying that?"

"When I made the decision to come here. I thought some of these stones might come in handy. Now, to enact this spell, we would normally use a white or purple candle. We have neither."

"Obviously." Margaret smirked.

"Sarcasm? Really, Tesoro?"

"Yeah. I know. Just go on."

"I'm hoping I can use the flames of the fire burning. I know it's a long shot, but if my ability is strong enough, maybe it'll work."

"You can do it. I know you can. Just believe in yourself as much as I do. And hurry. We're cutting it close."

Making a circle in the dirt around the outer area of the pool, he stood for a few moments and cleared his head. Envisioning a bright, white flame with his mind, Alex imagined it growing bigger and bigger until it filled the circle. Making the light as strong as he could, he held onto the image for a minute before sending the light into the crystal he held in his hand. Then he visualized the stone absorbing all the white light, growing more intense than a thousand flames.

Holding the stone to his forehead, he chanted the incantation:

"May the truth I seek be revealed to me, may the hidden come to light, so mote it be."

Stepping back from the circle, he closed it with the brush of his foot in the dirt. Once again removing the satchel, he wrapped the crystal in the white cloth and placed it back in the bag. Returning it to his pocket, he waited.

"Omg, look." Margaret's eyes widened.

Alex furrowed his brow. The scorched, brown bushes were not plants at all. Like thousands of pixels coming together, the truth revealed itself. Floating in the middle of the shallow pool of impure liquid was Bethany, Leon, and Roger.

"Alex!" Bethany screamed.

"Who the hell are you?" Roger sneered."

"Alex McKenna. I'm guessing you're Roger."

"That would be me. Don't move. I swear I will toss her into the first bolt that touches down." Roger crushed his arm around Bethany's neck.

"You sure do have an odd way of showing a girl you love her. From what I've been told, you tried to send her to *The Nowhere.* Now, you're willing to extinguish her life force for good? What the hell is it like if you *don't* like someone?"

"Come closer. I'll show you." Roger sneered.

"How did you find us?" Alex inquired.

"Hmm. Interesting question. Aren't you gonna ask how I escaped, *The Nowhere?*"

"I already know. You opened the door. You come from magick descent; you both do."

"Well. Aren't you the smart one?"

"I try," Alex said sarcastically.

"How did we find you? Leon, would you like to answer?"

"We followed Bethany's aurora. She left a trail of pink and purple crumbs. Like you said, magick background," Leon giggled.

"I didn't do anything. Alex, I swear," Bethany cried out.

"Stupid girl. Of course, you didn't do it on purpose. Roger put a honing spell on you months ago. We got it out of that book you stole," Leon barked.

"We didn't steal anything. You left it," Bethany replied.

"It wasn't yours to take," Roger roared.

"It's not yours either. It belongs in a secure place. It's dangerous in the wrong hands. Namely, yours," Alex deepened his voice.

Hearing the pleas from Bethany, the rest of the group swooped in and settled next to Alex and Margaret.

Sam swayed closer to Alex and whispered so Roger and Leon couldn't hear him.

"Alex. If any one of us tries to get to her, Roger *will* throw her in the path of the first bolt. He's not bluffing the guy is a real whack job. Even with teleportation, we'd never reach her in time."

"I got an idea. It's a little crazy, but I think if you really try, it'll work," Margaret whispered.

"Tell me." Alex leaned closer.

"Remember earlier how you were able to find Haven with everyone's help. Well, what if they help again. But this time, you concentrate on Roger releasing her."

"What are you saying?"

"We know you can move things with your thoughts in your sleep. Your mom said it's just a matter of time before you'll be able to do it when you're awake. Maybe now's the time. They can give you an energy boost, you just need to concentrate."

"It's not that easy."

"Maybe not. But what else do we got. If you get closer, he kills you and Bethany. I think it's the best plan right now." Margaret folded her arms. "Did everyone hear that?"

A low hum of confirmation answered the question.

"Hey. What the hell are you whispering about? You better not try anything." Roger shoved Bethany toward a bolt splintering through a low cloud. His arm still firmly gripped around her neck. "Next time, I'll let go and your girl will go sailing into her demise," Roger raved.

The group scooted close behind Alex. With their hands blocked from Roger's view, they each closed in, butting up to his back. His body jolted with the power unfurling in his veins. Concentrating his thoughts on the evil soul, Alex envisioned his own hand taking hold of Roger's forearm, he squeezed a tight grip and pulled back.

Roger must have felt something, he stiffened his grip around her neck, and squeezed.

"Oh. This is gonna be fun, McKenna. I guess there's more to you than I thought," Roger hissed. Maybe all those stories

I've heard about you have some truth to them. The dead are such gossipers."

Leon started to float toward Alex and the others.

"No. Stop. I want to see just what this breather can do. I'm intrigued." Roger snarled.

"Sam," Alex kept his voice in a low whisper, "As soon as I get Roger's hand to drop, you grab Bethany."

"Right on." Sam agreed.

Soaking in the intensity of the flames surrounding them, Alex drew on their hate. He filled every organ, muscle, and vein with it. Igniting an explosion that unleashed an inner beast. He no longer wanted to move Roger's arm, he wanted to rip it off. An impossibility, but a motivator. He glared at the billowing limb, imagining the sound of real flesh being torn from the muscle and bone. Blood spurting like a fountain on some ancient cobblestone in Italy. The more he could see the horror, the more he yearned for it. Bringing pain to Roger was now his sole purpose.

The darkness that took over didn't scare him as he thought it might. Rather, he embraced it, using it for his manipulation. His Gram had warned him about this. About letting in the dark magick that could only lead to no good. But he didn't have the time to worry about it. It was working. He could figure out how to intensify his light magick another time.

Slowly, finger by finger, Roger began to lose his struggle to remain tethered to his misguided love for Bethany. Alex was winning. Roger's hand loosened and then abruptly fell to his side.

"Sam. Go!"

Sam was at Bethany's side in the blink of an eye, just as a large bolt of lightning chopped overhead like blazing ax.

On instinct, while still connected to Roger, Alex directed his focus to the ghost and flung him like a baseball finding its way to a home run. With the crack of a ball kissing the bat, he catapulted him into the path of a blazing bolt and shattered the diabolical spirit into a thousand pieces. Glittering against the darkened gray sky, his remains shimmered to the ground, dissipating on contact.

Scouring the area for his second conquest, Alex spotted the frightened Leon trying to make his way around one of the turbid puddles of water. His left foot had sunk into the thick liquid, falling deeper with each attempt to free himself. By now the group had moved away, breaking their power bond with Alex. But it no longer mattered. The energy flowed free within him. Growing on its own, feeding off the emotions he had built. Turning in place to face the frenzied celestial, Alex imagined a thick rope with a large noose suspending over Leon's head. Dropping the noose around his neck, Alex's eyes filled with darkness as he slowly squeezed the circle tighter and tighter, until it secured a taut grip on Leon's neck.

With a wide grin, Alex raised the dangling boy straight up, nestling him between two plump, black clouds. The sharp, loud crack of a bolt striking in the distance indicated one would soon be close enough to finish the job.

"Alex. Stop it. You can't do this," Margaret pleaded.

She wrapped her arm around him, intertwining like a vine, lacing their bodies together. Tugging, Margaret tried to break his concentration.

Zachary moved directly in front of Alex. Catching his gaze and blocking his view of Leon.

"Alex. If you do this, you'll cross a line there's no coming back from. I know. I saw what happened to my mother. And the things my uncle did to some of those souls who were responsible for her death. It blackens your heart. Roger was one thing, he was going to destroy Bethany, but this is just murder."

"Alex. Please." Margaret's tears rolled down her cheek. A droplet landed on Alex's forearm and glistened in the tiny hairs on his skin. He wiped it away, the liquid moistening between his fingers. Looking up into her eyes, the sadness took his breath. *What the hell was he doing?* He looked away. Leon was still hanging in the space between sky and ground, screaming for help. A shaft of lightning torched the sky, it was close.

Margaret's whisper stroked the calm within his soul.

"Please. Alex." She gently kissed his lips.

Alex leaned into his beautiful girl and pressed his lips to hers with the intensity that had fueled his drive for justice. But this time, it was love that was the purpose. Love for her, for his family, and their lives. Darkness had tricked him into justifying his actions for the reason of good, no matter what the consequences. Luring him to the side that denied the light.

"I'm okay. It's over, I promise."

The noose disappeared from Leon's neck, releasing him. Not waiting to hear the reason he was spared, the boy disappeared.

"Let's find Haven," said Alex.

THE RESCUE

The lightning touched down, and shelter was the main concern. Zachary led them to a group of large boulders that offered a makeshift canopy. It wasn't the most secure place to wait, but it beats being out in the open. The sky had a wicked beauty as the strings of electricity sawed through the atmosphere, plunging to the ground, and scorching everything in its path. Each strike rumbled through the pit of Alex's stomach, churning the acid as they broke free and shot up to the back of his throat. The burning stung the thin layer of skin and he winced. Swallowing to push it back, the sour taste made him yearn for a peppermint. The little round disks of red and white that almost every candy dish contained around the Christmas holiday. *What he wouldn't give for one now.*

Reprieve came quickly when the lightning seemed to end in an accelerated timeline. Or maybe they were all just getting used to the pattern. Either way, he wasn't about to question it. Gingerly stepping to avoid the pitfalls of this gloomy terrain, Alex's attention was grabbed by the land on the far-right side of the river.

"Zachary. Did you ever wonder why the patches of land are in a diamond pattern?"

"Are you referring to the right plain?"

"Yes."

"If you see them from an aerial view, they are much like a drawing of the Kappa. Maybe it was a warning someone constructed a long time ago. However, if you are not above the ground, you cannot see the distinction."

"Weird," Alex sighed.

"Everything about this place is, as you say, weird. I have been to several in-between realms before I was a prisoner here. None of them, no matter how barren, compare to the stagnate world this is."

"When we first got here, we heard shrills coming from the right plain."

"Those are the souls trapped in the lair of the Kappa. Tortured before extinction. Sometimes they do hold a few for the benefit of luring other lost creatures into their clutches. Either way, you end up the same."

"Have the Kappa ever crossed plains?"

Zachary hesitated.

"They have. It is rare, but I have seen one or two."

"Wait. Did you just tell Alex there are Kappa here?" Sam's nostrils flared.

"He did," Alex replied.

"Dang it, what were you thinking, keeping this from us?"

"I thought if I mentioned it, it would just be one more thing for you to worry about. As I said, it is very rare. The chances of us seeing one is nearly non-existent."

"Yeah, well *nearly* doesn't mean never," Sam's snapped.

"We can't do anything about it now. Let's just be careful," said Alex.

"Can we stop flinging the testosterone and find Haven?" Margaret demanded.

"Your woman is aggressive, Alex," Zachary remarked.

"Hey, dead boy. I'm standing right here." Margaret pursed her lips.

"Yes, she is. And she can fight her own battles, so good luck." Alex grinned.

Alex soaked in the disdain of the realm. This is a place he would never forget. The crestfallen mountains stood like tall shadows hovering over every step, while the scattered splashes of sterile water and diamond patches of reaching flames seem to take solace in the impending doom that could be the group's fate. Calling to them, hoping at least one of the celestial energy or life force of a breather, would fall prey to the allure of the bright orange extensions, or murk of the deadly pool. Yearning to drain the vitality of either the living or the dead and feed its own hunger. Food was scarce in the Underworld, and each new entity brought an alert to the desolation.

Three more passes of lightning touching ground occurred before Zachary raised his right hand, indicating for everyone to stop. Positioned behind the curve of a large boulder at the base of the mountain, he stretched his neck to get a clearer view. Flowing just as he had described it, the black waterfall glistened as it ran from the top of the mountain into a pool of sparkling hues of purple. Pulling back, he dropped to the ground, using the mountain as a temporary shield. The team took the cue and sat next to him in a half circle.

"The shack of the Soul Gatherer should be around this mountain to our left. It is likely tucked behind a curtain of invisibility. I remember a large patch of land that has no fire or pools of water. It's butted up to the mountain, a perfect safeguard to limit access. If I'm right, that leaves us with the possibility of three entry points." Zachary swept his gaze over the treacherous land before continuing.

"We will need to stay clear of the black waterfall. We have

no idea if any Kappa might have wandered in and are hiding beneath the water. Since we are not able to visibly see it, we are going to have to break the spell and lift the curtain before we proceed. Alex, I need your help. I have rarely tried using my magick. It has brought me too much trouble, and avoidance was the logical course." He turned away from them. "Now, I have no choice. A spell is needed to break the illusion. I am hopeful your experience and energy will guide me. It worked when we opened the portal, a prayer to the gods we can repeat our success. Are you at ease with this?"

"I am. Anything you need to do to save Haven, I'm on board. But you're much more powerful than you know. I could feel your energy building the closer we got to this point. Your emotions are taking over, let the magick in you break free. All you need to do is concentrate. I can help guide you, but you need to trust in it. Own it and manipulate your energy, not the other way around. You're in control, not the magick or the darkness. If you focus on the light, good will come."

"Thank you. I shall need your assistance."

"You got it."

Alex extended his hand. Materializing to a solid state, Zachary reached out and took a firm grip. The boys shook on it. A bond was building between the two of them, and Alex knew once all this was over, it wouldn't be easy leaving their new friends.

"Alex and I will get closer to remove the spell. All of you stay here until you see the shack, then you join us. Once we are inside, Ophelia, your only concern is Haven. Amry, you assist her. Margaret and Bethany, check and see if there are other souls that need to be freed. Sam, you stay with us."

Amry stood. "I'm not trying to be a pain in the ass, but I'd like to go with you and Alex. Sam can go with Ophelia and

Bethany. This piece of work has made my friend miserable for decades, I want a little piece of him."

Zachary shook his head, "No. You are a woman, we do not need for you to be an added problem. We need the strength of men."

Margaret shot Alex a glare, this is exactly what their conversation was about earlier, only Zachary was in 16th century battle of the sexes mode. A time when females were helpless and obeyed. What little Margaret knew of Amry, she wasn't the type to be submissive.

"Amry's right." Alex agreed. "Things are different now, Zachary."

Zachary grunted but didn't argue.

"Wait. Shouldn't Alex stay with us. You know, being a breather and the possibility of being a permanent student at the Academy if something goes wrong." Margaret was in protection mode.

Alex took Margaret's hand and they walked a few feet away for privacy.

"Ciucciamia, I have to do this. Zachary's very strong, but he needs a guide to use his powers. I can help him. This is what I do. You know that. LaBoccetta's don't walk away from a fight, we run head on into it."

"Yeah. Well, you're also a McKenna and this is very dangerous."

"More dangerous than going toe to toe with two dark spirits, a maniacal old lady, and a demon that breaks through my living room floor from hell?"

Margaret turned away.

"I'll be all right. I promise." Alex brushed her hair from her shoulders.

"Again—don't die."

"I won't. You know, you say that to me a lot."

Margaret glared.

"Okay. I get it. No dying. I promise."

Joining the others, Alex sighed to himself. He made an impossible promise to the girl he loved.

"Zachary, we'll need a spell to break the veil. I know one if you don't mind."

"It was my hope you would." Zachary half-heartedly smiled.

The boys walked warily closer to the patch of barren land. Lining up with the center of the parcel, they raised both hands to release the magick to accomplish their deed.

"Repeat after me," Alex instructed.

"Moon and tide help me now, I seek the truth here not yet found, for underneath the fog there lies, the vision clears for open eyes. Peel back the veil from which it hides, show me the truth of what resides."

With each word that escaped from the lips of Zachary Abernathy, the half-dark sorcerer's intensity of powers grew. Small sparks pinged off his fingertips with the first sentence. By the spell's completion, balls of light circled the edges of his hands, illuminating the space around them. Alex widened his eyes, reveling in the magnitude of power his new friend possessed. Both boys repeated the spell.

The curtain slowly drew back. Peeling away like a page being torn from a book. Underneath revealed a small, wooden cottage with a thatched roof made from straw. The charm of smoke billowing from the chimney gave the look of a Thomas Kincaid painting, not the home of a soul stealing sorcerer.

The teens crept up beside the two boys, and the band of the living and dead enacted their strategy.

Zachary held on to the popping energy still coursing through his fingers. They would use it to knock down the door. Once inside, the two boys and Amry would focus on securing the sorcerer. If he's restrained, the rest of the plan should work—they hoped.

Crashing through the front door, Alex expected everything else but what was waiting. Sitting by the fire was an old man. His long gray beard draped down the front of his chest, like a bib. Thick, bushy, white brows canopied the pale blue eyes that were fixated on them. Alex pointed toward the stairs and Margaret slipped by with Ophelia, Bethany, and Sam.

"Alex, so nice to see you again. It's been so long. You were a baby the last time we met."

"You know him?" Amry turned to Alex.

"Never saw him before." Alex studied the old man.

"Ah. You don't remember. As I said, you were no more than two years old. How's your great grandmother? What a beautiful woman she is."

"I don't know who the hell you are, or if you really know my grandmother, but we're here to get Haven, and any other souls you've trapped."

"Nonsense. I haven't trapped anyone. They stay of their own free will."

"Really? Because it didn't look like that to me when I spoke to Haven the last time."

"An unfortunate misunderstanding. She's better now. They're all fine."

"Where is she?" Alex raised his voice.

"No need to get worked up. They're all upstairs. I'm sure your girlfriend will be reassuring you of their safety in a few minutes."

"Listen you waste of space, you tortured Ophelia and Haven for years. Keeping them apart ... you're the worst kind of evil. A despicable loser who preys on children." Army balled fists. "We're gonna send you to hell."

Amry lunged forward but the Soul Gatherer put his hands up, freezing her in place.

"Zachary, hold him!" Alex shouted.

Zachary rolled a ball of current between his hands and pushed it forward. It exploded in midair.

"Zachary, you will be a very powerful sorcerer someday, but right now your powers are wild and uncontrolled. Alex can help you a little, but neither one of you can match my millennium of experience. Let's not fight. Wait, you'll see everything's going to be fine."

The Soul Gatherer twinkled his fingers in the air, releasing Amry.

The thumping of footsteps drew Alex's attention toward the stairs. Margaret slid her hand down the top of the banister as she glided down, an enormous grin from ear to ear plastered on her face.

"Tesoro, where's the others?"

"They're upstairs resting. They needed to recharge."

"Did you find Haven?"

"Uh, huh. She's fine. They're all fine. It's lovely upstairs. Why don't you come up and see?"

"Not right now, my dear. But you go ahead and rejoin your friends. Alex will be up shortly." The old man waved his hand in dismissal.

Margaret turned around and proceeded to climb the stairs. "Wait, Margaret. Don't go up there."

Alex walked gingerly toward her. Placing his index finger under her chin, he looked into her eyes. His love was not in there.

"What the fuck did you do to her? Margaret—snap out of it!"

"She's happy. And you will be too. But first, I really would like to know how your Grandmother is doing. Did she finally drop that weak excuse for a husband?"

"You mean my great-grandfather?"

"No offense, but he really was a weight around her neck.

She had so much potential but traded it for that human. Well, I guess that's love."

"What's your name, old man?" Alex snarled.

"I believe all of you refer to me as the Soul Gatherer."

"Your real name."

"I guess it doesn't matter if I tell you. None of you are leaving this place. Vincenzo Fiorelli. Although I have no idea how that helps you. You said it yourself, you don't remember me."

"That's true. But my Gram will."

Vincenzo laughed from deep in his belly. "You are so amusing, Alex."

Alex clutched Margaret's hand, keeping her from going back to the second floor.

Vincenzo rose from his seat and carved through the air with the precision of a sharp blade. Hovering behind Alex, he leaned in close, his words grazed the teen's ears, stinging with every syllable.

"Get away from him!" Zachary yelled.

"Alex what did he say to you?"

"Candela strega, candela strega, luminoso di fuoco convocare gli spiriti per portare il mio desiderio. Candela strega, candela strega, lascia che la tua magia si leghi candela strega, candela strega, lascia che siano miei."

"What does that mean?"

"Witch candle, witch candle, bright of fire summon the spirits to bring my wish. Witch candle, witch candle, let your magick be tied. Candle witch, candle witch, let them be mine." Alex continued, "I believe that's the spell he's using to hold everyone here. They're in a trance. I think the only thing they feel is a love for him."

"So how come it's not working on you?"

"I don't know, and I don't care."

"You are a very special soul, Alex. My power is strong, you

surprise even me with your resistance. No worries. I'll just have to bind you to this realm."

Vincenzo mumbled under his breath, but Zachary was swift. Letting go of all his doubt, he allowed the fire to grow within. Sparks formed once again at the tips of his fingers, molding a large ball of white light. Pulling his right arm back like a pitcher on the mound, he released, sailing the energy right into Vincenzo's back. The force slammed him into the ceiling, dissipating his essence into a trail of smoke.

"We gotta hurry, this state won't last long for Vincenzo. Amry, go get everyone and bring them down here. Zachary, get ready with another blast. I think we're gonna need it." Alex directed.

"How can we get them to abide?" Zachary asked.

"I don't know yet. I'm hoping I can at least reach Margaret. If I can bring her back, she'll get them to move, I know it."

Zachary brought his hands within inches of each other. Circling them in small motions, he created another weapon of light. Locked and loaded, he waited.

Footsteps shuffling on the wood floor alerted Alex, and he ran to the base of the stairs. Ophelia was first, then Haven and Sam. Four other young, male souls trailed along with Amry at the rear. Alex recognized one of them, Leon.

He gathered them in a tight circle in the center of the room, to keep everyone in sight.

He approached Margaret. Her usual warm gaze was replaced by a cold stare.

"*Amore*, come back to me. You're stronger than this, fight it. I know you're in there, I know you hear me. I need you to push him out."

Margaret's expression remained void.

Alex moved in close, wrapping his arms around her waist, he whispered the words meant only for ears.

"I'll love you forever." He butterflied his way along the nape of her neck, across her cheek and then pressed a soft kiss on her lips. "If this is where I have to stay to be with you, then this will be our life together. A life without you, is no life for me."

Margaret folded like melting butter and Alex tightened his grip to hold her up.

"What happened?" Margaret groggily asked.

"You were under his spell. The one he used to hold Haven here. Are you okay?"

"I think so. I heard you. You were going to stay here with me."

"I'd never leave you. I thought you understood that."

"That's what brought me back. I was trying to fight him, but he was so strong. But the thought of you giving up your life, and you're after life, to be with me in this hell hole, no fucking way."

"I love you."

"You better," she whispered.

"If you're strong enough, we need you to take everyone out of here. I think once they're free of this place, the spell will be broken. I'm almost certain that's how Haven was able to reach me. Somehow, she must have managed to get out. His energy is tethered to this cottage. I can feel it. He draws them here, but this damn place is what fuels him, and gives him the strength. It's like it's alive. I'm beginning to think he's not a sorcerer at all. His powers are made from something entirely different. And if that's true, if we can destroy this house, then we should render his soul powerless."

Margaret took Haven's hand, and one by one, shoved the rest of the celestials out the front door.

"Remember, get them as far from this building as possible."

"I will."

Margaret held Alex's gaze as the door shut. "Now it's up to us."

A deep voice roared from the top of the stairs.

In the blink of an eye, Vincenzo was in the front room with Alex in his grip.

"Either one of you boys tries anything, and I will extinguish his life. Now leave. I'd like some time with Mr. McKenna, alone."

"You are severely mistaken if you think I would leave one of my friends with a lunatic like you." Zachary played with the lightening sizzling between his fingers.

"Well, I'm sure as hell not leaving either," Sam snapped.

"Zachary. Hit him with it." Alex nodded at the light growing in the sorcerers' hands.

"No, Alex. I can't hit him without getting you."

"It's okay, do it."

"I will not!" Zachary shouted.

"Alex, it seems your friends are not willing to listen to either one of us."

"Take me." Zachary fizzed out his weapon.

"Interesting. You're willing to trade yourself for a breather."

"What the hell are you doing?" Alex exclaimed.

"I am staying. Alex, you are the one leaving. This is the best choice. I have spent so many years here, in a way, the Underworld will be like going home. Vincenzo, take me. I will stay of my own free will. No spells."

"That is tempting. And I really wouldn't want a pissed off Mary LaBoccetta hunting me if she ever got wind I had her precious grandson. I will accept your offer."

"No! Zachary. We can do this. Just zap the bastard."

Vincenzo released his grip on Alex. Zachary smiled and came into solid form. Extending a hand, he reached for Alex. Once their grip was solid, Zachary drew him in for a hug.

Pivoting so Alex's back was toward the door, Zachary pushed him back. With a nod of the head, Zachary opened the door, and Alex flew out. Falling at the threshold, the door slammed shut before Alex could get up. A moment later, Amry's dazed spirit seeped through the sealed entry.

"Alex!" Margaret ran to his side.

"Where's Zachary?"

"He's still inside. He traded himself for me."

"What? No. We have to save him."

"We will. I just don't know how right now, and we're running out of time. We need to get you out of here before you become a permanent resident."

"Uh. Don't you mean us?"

"You know what I mean."

"I know you. So, get the idea out of your head. You're coming with me. If we can't get Zachary now, we'll come back. It will give us more time to figure something out." Margaret commanded.

"You're worried, I get that. But I'm not leaving without him. He spent five-hundred years here. And the only reason he's here now is because I asked him to help us. We need to figure something out. Sam, can you help me get that damn door open?

"Let's do it." Sam clenched both fists.

Sam shot up toward the roof and then circled twice. Blazing in fully charged, he shimmered into solid form seconds before slamming into the thick wood. The door burst, spitting splinters of wood everywhere.

Alex rushed in, once again face to face with the captor of souls. Zachary was tethered to a silver chain wrapped around an iron ring bolted to the wall.

"Alex, leave us." Zachary instructed, "I am bound to him with the eternity chain. You cannot break it. Please, just go."

"Not without you."

"Oh Alex. This could have been so easy. Now I'll have to keep you. There's no other option. Mary will come. But I have other places we can go. First, look at me."

"I'm not naïve, Vincenzo. I know how the spell works. I'm not becoming one of your drones."

Alex averted his eyes from the old man.

"Babe." Margaret stood in the doorway.

"Sam, get her away from here." Alex screeched.

Hoping the man's ego was as big as the crazy that occupied his mind, Alex tried distracting the maniacal thief with questions long enough for Sam to pull Margaret to safety.

"Vincenzo, I was wondering, how did you get the girls under your spell? You were down here with us, and they had gone upstairs."

"Over the years I've picked up a trick or two. The one I'm most proud of is my ability to astro-project. I can, in a sense, be in two places at once. You never know if you're really speaking to me, or— surprise."

Alex felt the feather of wind tickle the nape of his neck. Twisting to look behind, a second Vincenzo stood with another silver chain. The boom of the closing door pounded in Alex's head like a sledgehammer to brick. Without thinking, he spun around coming face to face with the doppelganger.

After the desperate Soul Gatherer repeated the spell that turned his victims into mindless zombies, he added, "Mr. McKenna, your will is strong. My spell had no effect earlier, but it will now."

Vincenzo opened his left hand, revealing a dollop of bright blue powder. Raising his palm, he puffed the substance straight into Alex's face.

"Stop. Let him go!" Zachary pleaded as he struggled to break free from his restraint.

Alex trembled. In his mind, he was pushed further and further back. Concealed behind an iron door with a peep hole the size of a candy bar. The outside world went about its business, while he was locked away. A back-seat driver to his own life.

The stench of mildew and earth, filled with death, surrounded him. Gagging, he struggled to take a breath. Pivoting around, it became clear where the vile smell was coming from. Locked with Alex in the iron clad room, were the bones and decaying bodies of Vincenzo's past victims. Souls that had forever lost their ability to remember who they were, permanently joined the Underworld.

Alex gasped when he recognized one of the many abominations piled on top of each other. Carol Bishop. The psychotic woman partially responsible for the death of Catherine and Ester, and the beginning of the Geranium Deaths. When a demon broke through the floor of his living room, swallowing her spirit like a midnight snack, he and his family assumed she had been obliterated from their world and any other. Apparently, they were wrong. He had no idea how she'd come to reside as one of Vincenzo's unwilling guests, nor did he care.

Pounding on the door, the fear rushed through his veins with the insanity of a feral cat. His mottled brain struggled to stay whole. Struggling to hold as pieces of his memory floated away, the shadows closed in.

"Alex! Alex! Come back! You stay with me!" Margaret screamed from the other side of the closed door.

"It is not working, Margaret. He is losing the battle," Zachary called out.

"Vincenzo, let him go. You have me, you said it yourself, you do not want his grandmother seeking vengeance from you."

"It seems Mr. McKenna is not going along with the plan. I gave him the chance, but he chose to come back. He sealed his own fate. Mary LaBoccetta will be for me to address when the time comes—if it comes. I will move us again and again; she will search hopelessly."

Trying to fend off what seemed inevitable, Zachary kept the insane Vincenzo engaged in conversation. Hoping if he bought them some time, his friends would come up with a rescue plan.

"I am befuddled." Zachary baited his captor.

"How so?"

"Why am I not affected by your spell?"

"I would assume the dark magick you possess won't allow such a spell to take over your mind. The benefit of being a son of the darkness."

"Alas, if I have all this dark energy, I should be able to break this chain you used to bind me. And yet?"

"Clever. I'm not naive. You thought I'd just give up my secrets, or rather, yours. You have so much to learn. Maybe one day you'll figure it out, but that's a worry for another time."

Zachary yanked on the chain, struggling to gain his freedom.

"Damn your blood. Let Alex and the rest of them go or I swear, when I do comprehend what I am truly capable of, you will be the first to experience my wrath."

"Says the boy chained to a wall," Vincenzo laughed.

"Sam. Take everyone and leave this place. Remember the pattern and head for the gateway. Use Leon to help you open it. We have to stay, but the rest shall be safe," Zachary demanded.

"No! I won't leave. Alex, you must hear me. I'm right here. Don't give in. You brought me out of it. You can do it yourself. I know you can. You're so much stronger than that prick. Fight!" Margaret sobbed.

"Sam, please save them," Zachary yelled.

Half-heartedly, Sam shimmied into solid form and

clutched Margaret's hand. Yanking, he pulled her through the threshold and slammed the door. She collapsed onto the dusty surface of the wood planks that served as a porch.

The rest of the group had regained full consciousness. The spell dissipated once they were on the other side of the cottage, just as Alex had hoped. Ophelia clutched a frightened Haven to her waist. She had finally gotten her little sister back, and she wasn't about to lose her again.

Margaret wiped away the tears streaming down her cheeks.

"Ophelia. Get Haven out of here. The rest of you go too. Leon, I hope we can trust you to do the right thing and get them home."

"You guys could have left me. After everything Roger and I did, you still rescued me. I'll open the portal and they'll be safe."

"Sam, keep your promise to Alex, lead them out of here. I'm staying." Margaret glared.

"Like hell you are. That promise included your safety too. I'm not going back on my word."

"You won't. I'm safe if I'm with him. Whether it's back home, or here in this damaged world, we stay together."

"Margaret ... " Sam pleaded.

"Go. Now. Don't let Zachary and Alex's sacrifice be for nothing," Margaret demanded.

"Stop arguing, the both of you. We need another plan. None of us are leaving anybody behind. Right?" Amry asked.

The teens nodded.

"Hey. Who is that?" Ophelia pointed.

The group turned and saw a figure emerging from the shim mering pool at the base of the black waterfall. Ophelia shuffled Haven behind her.

"Oh shit. Is that what I think it is?" Margaret questioned.

"It looks like one of those things that Zachary described." Amry backed up.

"A Kappa." Bethany's voice trembled.

"Leon you're with me. Margaret take everyone and hide." Sam instructed.

"Why do boys always think they have to be a hero? Besides, I'm capable of taking care of myself," Margaret snapped.

"Like you did with the Soul Gatherer?" Sam said sarcastically.

"That was fucking different, and you know it."

"Can we please save this for later? After we don't get murdered." Sam huffed.

"No. Margaret's right. We stay together. We're stronger as a whole," said Amry.

"Okay, I'm done arguing. If you want to risk your existence that's up to you. But let's get ready. Find anything you can use. A tree limb, a rock—anything. Margaret, we need you to understand, any one of us could teleport to another location in this garbage dump. But we stay for you and Alex. Don't do anything stupid to risk your life, and make this all for nothing," Sam warned.

"I get it. I'll be careful."

The beast grew larger with each step closer. The friends armed themselves with whatever they could find, and Ophelia hid Haven on the side of the cottage, behind dead vines creeping up a blacked-out window. Leon had come to his full senses while the other three unknown souls were still groggy. Amry handed them each a large rock and pushed them further back, towards the edge of the property and instructed them to stay put until they were needed. Hopefully giving them more time to regain full consciousness.

Margaret stiffened as the vision became clearer. The creature looked just as Zachary described it. A large hairy ape, with man like mannerisms, resembling drawings of the elusive creature, Bigfoot, which supposedly resided in the North-West states back home. The obvious difference was the bowl of water matching the circumference of its head, and the ear piercing shrills escaping its jaws.

Readied for battle, the friends stood shoulder to shoulder. Margaret's heart thundered alongside her veins like raging rapids, the roar was deafening. Squeezing her fingers around the solid piece of tree limb she was able to scrounge up, the only breather in the Kappa's path had no idea her hand had grown numb from the intensity of her grip.

"I thought Zachary said they trick you. This bastard is right out in the open. I don't get it," said Amry.

"We can worry about the why's later. Right now, " Sam swiftly turned around.

Creeping up from behind them, it's belly low to the ground, was a creature one could only describe as an escaped convict from hell. Large, thick horns pierced the scaly skin of its forehead, as they coiled upward, and ended in two points. The glow of its green eyes against fiery red skin could only hold the attention for so long, before its razor-sharp teeth, splintering through dry, cracked lips, stole the show. Moving in a giant lizard motion, its path was laid straight for the Kappa. Following several steps behind the crawler, was a young girl about seventeen or eighteen. A black strap clung to her left forearm, tethering the teen to the thick collar around the creature's neck. She kept the leash taut with a firm pull, as the beast tugged forward. Her blonde hair cascaded down both shoulders and halted just above her hips. Her body shimmered between the dimensions of whole and spirit, drawing attention to the sparkle of her limpid green eyes.

"Get out of my way! You're not gonna want to be in his path when I release the leash," the girl shouted.

They all scattered. Ophelia went to check on Haven and the others, while the two boys, Amry, and Bethany, took refuge by the front door. Margaret huddled by one of the four wooden posts holding up the roof of the porch.

The Kappa picked up momentum, breaking out into a full charge. Raising her arm, the girl released the strap, freeing the hellish beast. With the speed of a twisted dark spirit in the nightmare of your worst horror movie, the crawler skipped along the ground on all four limbs thriving in perpetual motion.

Ophelia rounded the corner with Haven and the other two spirits. Closing in with her friends at the front door, she reached out and took hold of Margaret. Tugging on the back of her hoodie, she pulled her into the circle. The dead surrounded the only breather, keeping her from harm's way, as best they could.

The two creatures collided creating a sonic like boom on impact. A fierce wind thrashed, claiming everything in its path. Fighting to hold on to each other, the teens anchored themselves to the framework surrounding the front door. Tightly closing their circle with Margaret in the center. The stranger was unaffected. She watched the battle from a large boulder at the base of the mountain, never once looking away.

Ripping at each other, their strength equally capable, the Kappa gripped one of the horns protruding from the hell creature's forehead, and bearing his long, razor-edged canines, he slowly tore the keratin away from the flesh. The creature's shrill roiled the acids in Margaret's stomach, sending them surging up to the back of her throat. Scorching the pipeline, she struggled to swallow and push the burning liquid back down.

With long claws, the hell creature struck back. Plunging them into the gut of the Kappa, it lacerated its belly before gashing open the wound from button to sternum. The Kappa took hold of the loose flesh on the nape of its opponents' neck and wrenched its head backwards. Wrapping its fingers along the row of bottom teeth, the Kappa cracked the creature's lower jaw, unhinging it. The cries of pain might have softened the heart if they weren't originating from two nefarious beasts.

Margaret held her hands to her ears, trying to block out the screams.

The stranger slid off the boulder and with the intensity of a steam powered engine, she raced toward the dueling demons of the Underworld. Twirling the black leash like a lasso, she rushed by the Kappa and let go of the leather strap. Shooting through the air, the noose found its intended victim. Wrapping around the Kappa's neck, it squeezed tight as the stranger pulled to secure the hold. Struggling to free itself, the Kappa was distracted and didn't see the hell creature circle around behind and reach for the bowl atop it's head. Using the tips of its claws, it sawed through the skin which bound the bowl to the Kappa's scalp. A thick, moss colored liquid gushed out like a geyser, covering the creature's face, and blinding it. With one last slice of its razor-sharp claws, the hell creature sheared the remaining slice of tissue and pulled the bowl from the Kappa's skull. Lifeless, the hairy beast fell to the ground.

The stranger knelt beside the wounded creature who had collapsed at her feet. Gently, she stroked the top of its head, until her soft hum lulled it to sleep. Straightening up, she walked toward the bewildered friends.

"Who are you?" Sam called out.

"I'm a friend," the stranger responded, "Or wasn't that obvious?"

"Sarcasm. I like her." Margaret smirked.

"How did you all get here?" the stranger asked.

"It is a very long story and we do not have time to explain. Our friends are prisoners of Vincenzo. We are trying to rescue them, but they're chained up. He has threatened to kill us if we interfere—it's our fault they are still in there." Ophelia curled her bottom lip.

"No. It's my fault. Everyone's here because of me," Haven whispered.

"Listen. It's no one's fault except for that weird lunatic in there," Amry argued.

"Amry's right. Let's just break down this door, get our friends, and boogie." Sam huffed.

"That's your plan?" The stranger baited.

"It's the best one we got," said Sam.

"No, it's not. It stinks. You're gonna wind up getting yourselves obliterated. And the breather here will become his pet. I've got a better plan."

"Who are you?" Sam repeated.

"No time. Here's what we're gonna do. The three zombies are more hindrance than help, we leave them, and the kid out here. Put them in the tree over there, they'll be safe. None of the creatures here can climb, not even the Kappa. Strange, I know. But that's how it is. The four cheerleaders will be a distraction. You knock on the door. Plead with the bastard to let you in, especially the breather. He'll be drawn to her lifeforce. Which by the way, it surprises me he let you go."

"My boyfriend's in there. He's a breather, and has paranormal abilities," Margaret explained.

"Ah. I get it. Okay. But still, you'll be enticing. You, Sam is it?"

Sam nodded.

"You and the other guy ... "

"Leon."

"You and Leon come with me. There's an entrance around the back, between the base of the mountain and the foundation. More like a crawl space. It leads to the basement. It's tight, but being spirits, we'll have no problem. I wish we could just materialize in the house, but you might have noticed you can't. The old man has a protection spell around the property. No shimmering in or out."

"Then what?" Sam inquired.

"Then we split up. You two go for your friends. I'll get the crazy soul steeler. There's a silver dagger in a wooden box on top of the mantle of the fireplace. That is the only thing, besides Vincenzo, that can break the chains that bind your friends. Get it, free them, get out."

"And what about you?" Sam asked.

"Don't worry about me. I'll restrain him as long as I can with my leash. My companion should be waking up soon fully healed. He'll find me if there's any trouble. You just get out of here. When you're safe, I'll find you."

Everyone agreed.

"Okay ladies, you're up." The stranger nodded toward the front door.

Margaret was the first to put her fist to the door. Pounding relentlessly until Vincenzo spoke up.

"You are trying my patience. I've been nice enough to let you leave. You should really go before my grace runs out."

"I'm not leaving without Alex. So, you either take both of us, or I'll find a way to knock this door down."

"Oh, very well."

Margaret stepped back when she heard the click of the latch unhinge. Amry glided in front of her, and Ophelia and Bethany stood on either side. She was cocooned in a circle of false safety.

"This is really noble of you to protect me, but who's gonna protect you? He can steal your energy just as easily as he can mine," Margaret whispered.

There was no time for a response. The door waved open, and Vincenzo stood in the archway with a wide smile on his face.

"Oh, how delicious. You've all returned. Where's my little lamb?"

"You will never get Haven again. But we are here of our own will," Ophelia snapped.

"Hmm. I guess that will be satisfactory. Although she *is* so young. Her energy is pure light. I'll miss it."

Ophelia struggled to maintain her composure. The thought of his vile soul being anywhere near her little sister stoked a fire in her belly that rose with every syllable that spilled from his lips. She bit the inside of her cheek to silence any words from slipping out. A breather trick she was happy to possess at the moment.

Vincenzo stepped aside, making room for the girls to enter. Alex was chained near the fireplace. Zachary was across the room in a simple wooden chair. Margaret glanced over at Amry, who had clearly spotted the same prize she had. Her wide eyes were fixated on the small wooden box, placed in the center of the mantle. The girls exchanged a slight drop of the chin to signify they were in unity.

"Mr. McKenna, I release you."

Alex startled back to reality when the mental iron door abruptly flew open, freeing his mind from captivity. Dazed for only a moment, clarity flooded in when he saw Margaret in the room.

"What the hell are you doing here, get out." Alex shouted.

"You stay, I stay." Margaret tightened her fists at her side. She swore if it were possible, Alex would have steam rising from his nostrils. The pissed off look combined with the confusion of desperation in his eyes, threw her o balance for a moment. She would explain everything once they got out of there—all of them.

"Now then. Why don't you three souls go upstairs. I'd like to have a moment with Miss Margaret."

"We stay together. We're here, but we 're not gonna be your zombies. You'll have us, but as we are," Amry proclaimed.

"I don't know whether your obstinance is charming, or just a huge pain in the ass. Sit. All of you."

Margaret locked eyes with Alex. She hoped his *spidey sense* would pick up the real reason they were there. This was a rescue plan. No one was about to lay down for the diseased spirit of the Soul Gatherer. If he were to remain alone for eternity, it wouldn't be enough time.

"So how does this work? We take turns being your energy bitches. You cook dinner, and we sit around the table discussing our day? What the hell do you plan to do with all of us?" Margaret barked.

"Attitude, Miss Margaret."

"Stop referring to me as Miss Margaret. I'm not a debutante. In fact, I prefer you didn't say my name at all. Hey you will work just fine."

"I can see you're going to be fun. Full of energy." Vincent licked his upper lip.

"Oh, you're so gross." Margaret winced.

"Gross? That's putting it mildly. If I could, I'd throw up. What about you Lia? You feel the stomach bubbling?" Amry glared.

"Bubbling and sloshing to nauseating levels of disgust." Ophelia furrowed her brow.

Amry glided next to Alex.

"How does it feel Alex? Margaret loves you so much she's willing to give up everything for you."

Margaret narrowed her eyes and pursed her lips. Amry inconspicuously wiggled her hand indicating more. Confused, Margaret widened her eyes.

"Does it make you happy, Alex? The fact that her love runs so deep?" Amry coaxed him on.

"Amry stop it," Alex commanded.

"I mean, she was free. And yet, here she is, with you."

Alex's eyes grew dark, his complexion beamed like Santa's

red suit at the Macy's Christmas Day parade. His nostrils flared, and both fists were clenched at his side.

Margaret's cheeks grew full of the wide grin sparkling across her face. It became clear that Amry's strategy was to get him angry enough to rile up his abilities. Alex's gifts ran on emotions. The stronger they were, the stronger he was. *Maybe they could tap into his newfound use of telekinesis.*

"And look at you. Chained up, and unable to help her if you tried. That chain looks damn solid. I bet there's no cutting through that," Amry egged him on, "So what's the plan Alex? Because the others you've had worked out so beautifully. What was it you said? Oh, I remember. We just need to trust you. Look what that's gotten us. Eternity with this dreadful man, in a shit-hole world of desolation and torture. Great plan. I can hardly wait to see what else you have in store for us."

The words plunged into Alex's chest like a steel dagger. The fire in his belly grew to an inferno, as he heard Amry's insults repeat over in his head. Stealing a glance at Margaret, her eyes were like saucers and glued to the small wooden box on the mantle. Alex raised a brow and she ping-ponged her gaze from him to the box and back again. He wasn't sure of its importance, but it was enough to monopolize Margaret's attention.

Amry dug into him again.

"I wonder what your families are going through right now. Not knowing where you are, and not to mention what it's gonna be like when you don't return. When a mother loses a kid it's like hell on earth. I know, I watched my mom's soul die a little each day as I got worse."

The roar that escaped through the unhinged jaw of Alex McKenna, came from deep in his belly. Rising into his chest cavity and escaping with all the intensity of a lion claiming his territory. Alex whipped his head around focusing on the box. With merely a thought, he pulled the box from the mantle and into his hands. Directing his rage into the grip, crushing it like a piece of cardboard, the dagger fell to the floor. Margaret quickly swooped it up and cut Alex's chain. Scrambling to Zachary's side, she sliced him free with one thrust.

Vincenzo had no idea what had just happened. He circled around the room like a child in search of their mother.

"No. You'll ruin everything!"

He called out the same spell that held them captive earlier, but his words were halted when Alex raised a bent arm and released it—sending Vincenzo flying to the other side of the room.

"I guess we're a little late to the party," the stranger proclaimed.

"Ruby?" Zachary called out.

"Zach?"

"What? How? I thought you were dead. I saw the Kappa take you."

"No time for explanations. Let's finish this, and I'll tell you everything."

"You little tramp! I should have squeezed the life-force out of you right from the beginning." Vincenzo lunged for Ruby.

"You sard, get away from her!" Zachary commanded.

The room filled with thick, black smoke. Circling the floor until it found its intended, it wrapped around the bottom of Vincenzo's feet, trellising his torso in a tight cocoon, before seeping into his mouth and silencing him.

Margaret ran to Alex's side. "Alex, what are you doing?"

"That's not me. I think it's Zachary."

The dark magick oozed from Zachary's fingertips like honey dripping off a hive. Soon every corner of the room was drenched with a sticky, black substance. The celestials hovered above the muck and carried Alex and Margaret with them.

Ruby took hold of a piece of the silver chain that had fallen to the ground and circled around Vincenzo several times. She securely tied the ends in a knot, incapacitating their former captor.

The smoke reduced to a fine mist before escaping through the gap in the bottom of the front door.

"Time for your story to end, Soul Gatherer." Zachary took Ruby's hand. "Shall we send him someplace he will never bother anyone again?"

"That sounds lovely. Got somewhere in mind?"

"As a matter of fact, I do."

"Wait," Sam interrupted, "You're not going to extinguish him?"

"If I use the darkness for evil, and that is what I would be doing if I drain him, then I become evil. That is exactly what the demons who hunt me are wishing for. Alex was right. If I use my magick for good, no matter if it comes from the darkness, the light will win."

"Do you understand, Sam?" Alex asked.

"Yeah. I get it. I just wish he could suffer like he made Haven and Ophelia suffer all these years. Not to mention all the other souls he's taken hostage. I wonder how many of them he spared, like you're sparing him."

"I promise you Sam, he will suffer. This will be far worse than disappearing," Zachary continued, "Alex, can you help me?"

"Sure. But I have no sorcerers in my bloodline."

"I think your abilities will be enough. It is a long family line of what did you call it, *spidey sense*? Sounds like magick to me. You ready?"

"What are you two doing?" Margaret whispered.

"You'll see," Alex murmured.

Suspended back to back, the two boys raised a hand to the fireplace and the other to Vincenzo. In unison, they recited the spell to send him to a fate worse than complete obliteration—an infinity of torture.

"One to open, one to close, to do it again, no one knows. For one soul, the course is true, darkness comes, it's different for you. One to close, the deed is done. Never ending, *The Nowhere* won."

"Nooooooo!" Vincenzo screamed.

The hearth unhinged, opening its fiery mouth to reveal a rotting arm. The flesh eaten monstrosity, slithered along the barren floor, like a serpent clinging to the asphalt on a warm summer's night. It coiled around Vincenzo's legs, squeezing the Soul Gatherer before he had a chance to escape. With the elasticity of a well-worn rubber band, it stretched itself up toward the face of the whimpering soul. Opening its fist, the anomaly revealed a hollow tunnel inside the decrepit arm, it capped the terrified Vincenzo's head, and swallowed him whole. Retreating, the abomination passed through the gateway of the waiting hearth and disappeared.

"Where did he go?" asked Ophelia.

"To *The Nowhere*. His eternity of hell." Zachary grinned. "Now can we all get out of here and back to the Academy? I bet Headmaster has the entire school searching for us by now."

Amry opened the door.

Zachary drifted to Ruby and wrapped his finger around hers. "Now, tell me what happened. If I thought for one second you were still alive ... Ruby, I am so sorry." Zachary looked down.

"Hey. Hey. You had no way of knowing I wasn't dead. When the Kappa took me, I thought I was gone too. But my little friend here saved me."

The creature moped over to Ruby and nestled along her ankle. She reached down and stroked his back. Its purr was like that of a large feline.

"You're healing nicely," Ruby cooed to the creature.

She inspected the spot where the Kappa had ripped off its horn. A small nub had replaced the gaping wound.

"I assumed all the beings indigenous to this land were monsters." asked Zachary.

"He may not be the prettiest thing to look at, but he's no monster. If it weren't for this guy, I'd have been obliterated long ago. He's been at my side since the first day we met. Well, I ran, he chased me. I had no idea he was just looking for a friend. When you see a giant lizard beast, belly to the ground, and rushing toward you, you tend to not wait to say hello."

"How did you know he would not bring you harm?"

"Like I said, he saved me. So, there was that. Then I realized as I was running that he could've easily caught up with me, and he didn't. He wasn't chasing me; he was following me. Giving me space to figure it out. There's definitely a language barrier, so discussion was out of the question. But I've learned much of his body language over time, and now we communicate just fine. He's my everything here." Ruby smiled.

"If he's so friendly, why did you have him on a leash?"

"That was for his safety. If he would have gone for the Kappa near water, there might have been more of them hiding. I just kept him leashed until I knew he'd have an equal shot."

"Do you think he understands the nature of our conversation?"

"I guess some words have become familiar to him, but the full scope of what they actually mean, I'm not sure. Why?"

"I feel regretful for grouping him into the monster category." Ruby chuckled.

"No worries. I doubt he knows that word. He's never heard it from me."

"Does he have a name?"

"Don't laugh. Promise?"

"I promise."

"Nothing ever seemed to really fit him, and since I

couldn't ask him what his name was, I just started calling him —Spot."

Zachary struggled to hold in the laughter. He clasped both hands over his mouth.

"Hey—you promised."

"Spot? You have been imprisoned here all this time, and the most creative name you could formulate was, Spot?"

Everyone roared with laughter.

Spot peered up at Ruby and then rubbed his side across her calf.

"Don't worry, they're not laughing at you. They're laughing at me."

They abruptly stopped.

"He understood that?" Zachary whispered.

"Not so much what you said, but the laughter probably set him off balance. He's not used to all of you, and he's probably trying to figure you out."

"Hells bells. I'm so sorry."

"We all are," Amry apologized.

"It's okay. We're all just getting to know each other," Ruby soothed.

"There will be plenty of time for that once we get back to the Academy," Zachary chimed in.

"Zach, I'm not going back. I mean, I'd love to. In fact, there's nothing I'd want more. But I can't leave him here alone. He's the only reason I'm still sane."

"You cannot be serious. If you stay here much longer, you will never be able to return. He might keep you sane, but you will spend eternity in the Underworld."

"I'm okay with it. I made my peace a long time ago. This place, as much as it is a rat's hole, and it is definitely a rat's hole times one hundred, it's home now. Spot can't come back with me. What would everyone say? Your uncle? Do you think for a second he'd let him stay at the Academy?"

"I do. He thinks you gave up your life-force for me. He feels guilty enough about me being lost for all those years. He will not question this. I know it."

Zachary slowly reached down and gently glided his hand over Spot's back. The creature arched up and then collapsed to the ground. Rolling to one side he waited.

"Oh, I see. You want me to scratch your belly. I can do that."

Zachary shimmered into solid form and stroked his hand over the docile creature's tummy. Spot hummed a low, grave melody, as he wiggled with happiness.

"See. We are already friends. Please Ruby, come with us. The both of you. If it does not work out, I promise I will bring the two of you back here myself."

Ruby looked away, and then back at the teens waiting for an answer.

"You're all so close. I saw how you watch out for one another, it's like Spot and me. If the Headmaster did agree, it would definitely be a much better life for the both of us." Ruby smiled.

"Of course, it would. And I am fairly certain the students at the Academy would love to have a demon-looking, lizard-like creature at their school. Spot will make a plethora of new friends —right after they get over the initial shock." Zachary grinned.

"True. And Spot can offer added protection for you. I think your uncle will love that." Ruby turned to her loyal companion, "What do you say my friend, you want to go and explore a new realm?" she patted Spot's horn.

The creature gazed up and rolled over onto his feet. He took two steps and joined Ruby by her side.

"I guess he's in. We both are." Ruby nodded.

"Now let us leave this place. We have about five minutes before the next lightning ground strike," Zachary instructed.

"I'm confused." Margaret held up her hand. "I thought *The Nowhere* was the only realm that had designated portals. You said the in-betweens can be opened from anywhere."

"They can. But you must return to the port from which you entered to reach your original destination. It is much like walking through a doorway in your home, if you want to enter the kitchen you go through the kitchen door. We started at point A to get to point B. We need to get back to point B ..."

"To get to point A, again. I get it." Margaret tapped her head.

"Zach, you can get us there," said Ruby.

"Rube, I haven't even begun to figure out this dark magick. What I've done so far is nothing. Mistakes at best."

"You just gotta concentrate. See what you want, and it'll come to you."

"How do you know? Are you suddenly an expert in the darkness?"

"No. I've just learned a lot living in this place. The souls I've met over the years have taught me so much, some of it I wish I could forget," Ruby continued, "but if you don't want to try, we'll take our chances with the lightning. I mean you got everyone here. How long did that take?"

Zachary brushed his brow. "I understand."

"Focus on what you want."

Zachary glanced at the group of teens in front of him, then closing his eyes he saw the doorway to the portal in his mind. One by one, he brought each one of them to the opening.

"I do not think this will work," Zachary sighed.

"Open your eyes, Zach," Ruby giggled.

Fluttering his lids, Zachary slowly opened his eyes. In front of him was the gateway to the portal, and the gang was standing beside him.

"I did it." Zachary's eyes widened.

"Told you. Just believe in yourself. There's so much more you're capable of. But for now, how about you just get us home." Ruby grinned.

"Alex, a little help? I could use some of that *spidey sense?*" "For the record, *spidey sense* is all Margaret's words. My family refers to our gifts as the *know.*"

"Really, Alex? Right now, is when you think it's time to have the label discussion?" Margaret shook her head.

"No. I mean, you know I love your reference. It's just, I wanted him—them, to ... never mind. You're right, it's stupid. Sure, Zachary. Let's get everyone home."

The two boys lined up directly in front of the unseen doorway in hopes of unlocking the portal again. Arms stretched out in front of them, they recited the chant in unison. A burst of wind followed by a lustrous twirl of colors, the bridge to the Academy was open.

"You take them out of here, Zachary. Margaret and I will follow."

"No. I think breathers first."

"We're fine. Go."

Zachary's brow furrowed. "All right, everyone through. Ophelia and Haven, you go first. Come, we do not have much time. The vortex will not stay open for long. You hear me, McKenna?"

"I hear you. We'll be right behind you."

Alex pivoted in place. Soaking in the landscape of burning fires, shadowy waters, and the bleak life of the Underworld, he wanted the picture to be stored in his memory. A reminder of the dismal fate that could befall a lost soul, and the job he knew he needed to continue. Grabbing Margaret's hand, he tightened his grip.

"Ready?"

"Sure. But was that?"

"I wanted to make sure I remember why me and my family do what we do."

Margaret gently squeezed his hand and smiled.

With two quick steps, they leaped into the twisting wind, and the pathway back to the Academy of Souls.

THE PLAN WAS to head straight to Abernathy's office. Zachary figured his uncle would have the entire security team on the case by now. Mr. Rain and Mr. Coal were surely leading a brigade of overzealous celestials, armed with low level sorcerer powers, ripping apart the campus one room at a time, searching for him. And then there would be the explanation of their new guest, the attention grabbing, Spot. Explanations were going to have to be good.

Since teleportation would be the fastest and easiest way to get Spot there unnoticed, Alex and Margaret planned to meet the rest of them at Abernathy's office. They agreed it no longer mattered if the students realized they were breathers; it was kind of a moot point.

"Damn. I wish we could teleport like them. I want to know what it feels like to pop in and out at will." Margaret smirked.

"You did, sort of."

"What do you mean?'

"When Zachary brought us to the portal. It was by magick, but I'm thinking it's probably pretty similar."

"Nope. That was like hitching a ride. I want to drive." Margaret kissed his cheek.

Walking along the cobblestone path to the courtyard, Alex soaked in what he knew would be his last day at the Academy. Peering up at the roof of the main building, students sat with their feet dangled over the side, sharing a discussion with an open book suspended in front of them. Over in the large oak tree, at the very top, and partially hidden in the leaves, a young couple sat kissing. Alex turned his gaze toward the sky. Golden rays pierced through a cluster of stark, white clouds, illuminating four students nestled on the aerial puffs of faux cotton.

"This wouldn't be awful," Alex commented.

"What wouldn't be awful?" Margaret questioned.

"The Academy. To wind up here. I mean if you have to have a depot, this would be the one."

"Open your eyes."

"What do you mean?"

"Alex. You're not seeing the whole picture. Every one of them lacks the sparkle of excitement, enthusiasm, hope. They're complacent, not content. There's a reason that each one of them came here. The Academy isn't a vacation destination, it's sort of an in-between. It may look cool, and feel homey, but it's still just a place to go because they're lost. Each one had their own reason, but the fact remains, they can't be with their family, friends, lover—they're stuck."

He took another long look. This time, he peeled away the colored lenses he used to see the Academy. A peaceful, soulful place in the afterlife. But Margaret was right. The harder he looked, the more he noticed. These kids weren't home, they were at the bus stop waiting for someone to pick them up. The problem was it was all inside them. They're the only ones who had the power to move on, but they had to figure it out. What if it took years? What if they never figured it out? Suddenly the beauty of the Academy faded away to desperation.

"You're right, their journey is only half over." He intertwined his fingers with hers. "I love you; I couldn't do this without you."

"Don't worry, you won't have to. I'm not going anywhere." She pressed her forehead to his.

When they reached the Headmaster's office, Abernathy was seated behind his desk. The rest of the teens were scattered on the floor, and Spot lay on his belly in the center of the room, Ruby by his side.

"Ah, Mr. McKenna and Ms. Margaret. So glad you could finally join us. I hear you co-hosted your little outing today with my nephew. Please, have a seat." Abernathy pointed to the floor.

Alex leaned in and whispered into Zachary's ear, "How come the place isn't in total panic mode looking for you?"

"My uncle said time moves differently in the Underworld. It may seem like hours or days, but here at the Academy it has only been a few minutes."

"Huh. Cool. That's good for me and Margaret. Buys us a little more time before we need to leave."

"I've listened to my nephew's explanation of this debauchery today, and now I'd like to hear your version, Mr. McKenna." Abernathy sat back in his chair.

"It's pretty cut and dry. We knew we had to rescue Haven, before it was too late, and Ophelia lost her forever. If not, Ophelia would be at the Academy for eternity because she would never be able to forgive herself for Haven's fate. So, instead of losing two souls, we gained six. We were able to rescue Ruby, Leon, the other three teens and Spot. Oh, and defeat Roger and Vincenzo for good. All in all, it was a pretty good day." Alex grinned.

"A pretty good day, you say. From where I'm sitting, you and my nephew put everyone's eternal life at risk. Not to mention bringing this creature into the Academy. What are we supposed to do with it?"

"I know you're upset, Headmaster. But we had no choice. As for Spot, he's a great protector and Ruby has him eating out of her hand. He could only be an asset when it comes to defeating the goons looking for Zachary. Which, that's another plus. Zachary was able to use his dark magick but tap into the light. So, lesson learned today." Alex squirmed.

Abernathy narrowed his eyes.

"You know, I think it's time Margaret and I head home. We don't want to miss our window. This is a great school you created, but we don't belong here."

Abernathy cleared his throat. "Wise words, Mr. McKenna."

"Uncle, can we go? I think everyone would like to say a proper farewell."

Abernathy stood and folded his arms. "Go. But Zachary, you come back later. We still have some things to sort out. Miss Ruby, you and Spot can stay for as long as you'd like. If you should find the light waiting for you, know we will take good care of your creature."

"Thank you, Headmaster. But I think I'll be sticking around for a while." Ruby glanced at Zachary.

"As for you Leon, feel very lucky that everyone here has forgiven you. You will remain on a trial basis. But I warn you, one more misguided act, and I will send you to *The Nowhere* myself. Now get out of here, all of you. Oh wait. One more thing, Mr. McKenna. Please, do tell your grandmother I send my warmest regards."

Alex reluctantly curled the corner of his mouth. He wasn't sure exactly what that meant, but whatever it was, it felt like a stiffly starched shirt on a hot August day.

Leon and the other two teens they saved from the clutches of the Soul Gatherer, were sent to the office of the psychiatrist, Dominique Dunworthy, for evaluation. Ruby and Spot left to explore their new home, while the original band of after-life detectives, plus two breathers, chose walking as their mode of transportation to Ophelia and

Amry's dorm room. The place where the Academy adventure began.

Once the door behind them closed, the group huddled close.

"Alex, thank you so much for helping me find Haven. I could never repay you for what you have done. You too, Margaret. If you both didn't come to help, I don't know what would have happened."

"You owe us nothing. This is what my family does." Alex smiled.

"We're going to miss you two. You're okay—for breathers," Sam laughed.

"I know I haven't said much, but I really am glad I got to meet you both." Bethany grinned.

"Yes. Without you, I would not have been able to open the portal. We make a good pair, like brothers, McKenna." Zachary smiled and turned away.

Amry circled around Alex, shimmered solid and then gently kissed his cheek.

"Thank you, for helping my friend and her little sister." Her green eyes twinkled for the first time since Alex and Margaret arrived. Amry was—happy.

"I guess we should go. We love all of you, if you ever need me, you know how to find me. Ophelia, I hope you and Haven can find your family now. Amry, maybe this will be your ticket to the light too, knowing Ophelia is okay. Sam and Bethany, I'm not sure why you're still here, but I have an idea." He gazed over at Margaret. "I believe that if you love someone, the one that shares not only your heart, but your soul, you will be together forever. In this life and beyond. I hope that helps."

"Groovy. Thanks, Alex. I hope so." Sam wrapped his arms around Bethany's waist.

"You know there is something I wanted to ask your uncle, but I forgot." Alex said.

"What's that?"

"The spell to open *The Nowhere,* it didn't make sense to me. *One to open, one to close.* I get that part. It signifies it takes two souls to initiate and close it. But...*to do it again, no one knows. For one soul, the course is true.* That part is boggling my mind. I was gonna ask him before we left, but I forgot."

"I can explain it to you. My uncle told me that it means the realm changes every time someone enters it. So, *The Nowhere* for you, is different than *The Nowhere* for me. That's why the course is true. It is the true fear that everyone possesses. It cannot be duplicated, and no one else knows your true fear but you."

"Ah. Now it makes sense. That means eternity in complete solitude with your worst fear. That is hell."

"Indeed. And that soul stealing bastard will know his forever."

"Thanks, Zachary. This was a wild experience. Although, when I tell my Gram, she'll tell my mom, and I think I'll probably be grounded until college. But it was worth it." Alex smiled.

"Alex, a little help?" Zachary beamed.

The boys raised their arms together for the last time, reciting the spell to open the portal to the living world.

Tightly holding on to each other, Alex and Margaret bid their final good-byes, and stepped through the passage home.

LIFE GOES ON

It had been two weeks since Alex McKenna and Margaret had come to the Academy. Ruby and Spot were the talk of the school. Especially Spot. He seemed to love his newfound attention. It was Friday night and the theater played the comedy, Ghostbusters. A fun poke at every cliché the living world thought being dead was all about. Ophelia couldn't wait to take Haven. She had never seen a motion picture and she knew her little sister was going to freak with excitement. The theater was empty. Although the film appealed to the band of diabolical-soul slayers, the rest of the students, not so much. They didn't find the humor in the exaggeration of the paranormal quite like Ophelia, and the rest of them did.

The gang was meeting in front of the theater at six o'clock. Amry had a few projects she had wanted to finish first, so she was coming straight over from the library. Sam and Bethany had been spending more alone time together. Ophelia thought it was because they were about to decide. Alex's words had really struck deep in Sam's core, and they had a long discussion about it after science class. Sam had confided in her, his wish to take the light. He was still scared, but he felt better after hearing Alex's take on it.

Zachary had been making up for lost time both with his uncle, and Ruby. His powers were growing more each day, and although he struggled with the darkness, Ruby was there to kick him in the ass and remind him what side to tap into.

Ophelia had taken Haven to the library. They were there for nearly the entire day. When they left, Amry was finishing up and promised to join them shortly.

Arriving at the theater, Ophelia pulled open the large, heavy doors, and Haven laughed at her big sister.

"What's so funny?"

"You, silly. Why do you open the doors when we could walk through the walls? Or better yet, teleport inside from the library."

"I enjoy the entire experience. If I teleported everywhere, I would miss everything around me. If I walked through walls, I couldn't feel the texture of the door in my hand. All of it is an experience that should be treasured. The next life will come, and we will leave all of this behind. I'm sure it will be wonderful, but it will be different. Understand?"

"Uh, huh. I do. All that time I was away from you, I never wanted to think about where I was. It just made me sad. But this place is so nice, I want to feel everything, too."

"Haven. Can you still feel things?"

"What do you mean?"

"Do you feel pain, or the warmth of the sun?"

"No. Why?"

"When we had our beginning, I wasn't supposed to start mine yet. Because I left too early, I have kept certain things that are still like the breathers. I'm noticing lately though, that they are starting to dwindle. Do you know I used to take a shower every morning since I arrived here?"

"Really?"

"Yup. But since we've gotten back from the Underworld, I have not had the urge. I haven't felt a lot of things I did before."

"What do you think it means?"

"I don't know. Hey, look. There's Bethany and Sam. Let's go sit by them."

The sisters flowed toward the couple.

"Amry's not with you?" Bethany asked.

"No. She is still at the library. She will be here soon." "They're about to start the movie," Sam whispered.

"It's okay. She's seen it at least ten times." Ophelia smiled.

Ophelia took Haven's hand and they rose up toward the ceiling, stopping at perfect eye level with the screen.

"This is the best seat in the house."

Haven squealed. "This is perfect!"

Down below, Bethany and Sam waved to them.

The expression on Haven's face was priceless when the movie started. She kept reaching out for the screen, trying to touch the characters. Mesmerized by the enormous picture in front of her, and the idea that they could trap people on a reel of film, and then send them to the screen. Of course, Ophelia had to explain that wasn't what happened. The reality didn't seem to sway Haven at all. She was still just as captivated with Ophelia's truth, as her own make-believe reasoning.

The movie was about half over and Ophelia started to worry. Amry hadn't shown up yet. She asked Sam and Bethany if they wouldn't mind watching Haven. No reason to take the little girl away from her enjoyment. They happily agreed.

Ophelia left the theater through the doors but once outside, her anxiety caused her to toss aside her need to soak in the experience of life at the Academy. In two shakes, she was standing at the help desk of the library. Amry's books were still strewn across the table, but she was nowhere in sight. Creeping toward the disturbing scene, she noticed a small white sheet of paper on the top of a pile of neatly stacked books. They were set on the table directly in front of the pulled-out chair.

Twenty minutes earlier

Amry shivered. A cool breeze brushed along her shoulders. Startled, she set her book down. She hadn't felt a sensation like that in years. In fact, not since her beginning nearly forty years ago. Her chest heaved as her breath sawed in and out, and the faint thump of a heartbeat whispered its way to her ears. Legs trembling, she stood. *What the hell is happening to me*? She thought. A flutter of anxiety wrapped itself around her owing body, quickly she turned around, sensing something or someone behind her.

A small ball of light hovered in the space between the ceiling and the floor. With each beat of her newly found heart, the ball grew larger. Opening like a flower on the morning of a Spring day, it revealed a shadowy dot in the center. Moving toward her, the shadow took over the center of light. From dot to silhouette, the closer it became, the more it revealed.

Amry gasped when the vision became clear. Stepping from the light, emerged a young man about nineteen or twenty. Average height, dark wavy hair and intense brown eyes. Stepping back, she nearly fell over the chair, and struggled to gain her footing.

"I see some things never change." His deep voice melted her heart like the morning frost on a sunny day.

"John? Is it you?"

"My love, my heart. I've waited for you for such a long time." The young man extended his hand and Amry shyly took it.

"What's happening? Why do you look so young?"

"I'm here to bring you across the light. So many times, I'd

hoped you might come, but I knew you'd never leave, not until Ophelia found Haven."

"How did you know?"

"I would check in on you from time to time. I've missed you so much."

"John. What happened to you? You still look like you did the day I left."

"I took ill about a year after I lost you. It was okay. I couldn't bare living my life without you in it."

"No. No. It wasn't supposed to happen like that. You were supposed to get married, have children, grow old. The thought of you living a full life is part of what kept me going all this time. To think you were waiting, and I stayed here."

"You stayed for your friend. You're not the kind of person who'd abandon someone. I knew that. But we're together now. For eternity."

He scooped her up into his arms, capturing her lips, he released the curbed emotions of the past forty years. Amry's passion swirled, bringing back every memory they shared together. His voice beat along her veins with the syllables *I love you*, whispered in her ear.

Tears spilled from her eyes, trickling down along her cheek to her quivering lips. She could taste the salty liquid, and for the first time since her beginning, she felt human. John moved along her jawline, and down to the nape of her neck. Showering every inch with a soft kiss. She collapsed in his arms, giving herself completely to the man she had loved since the moment they met.

Gently, he pulled back and brushed her ears with the words she'd been longing to hear for years. "It's time, my love."

Amry looked longingly into his eyes. She couldn't believe this was happening. And then it slipped into her thoughts, pushing away the joy. *What about, Lia and Haven?*

"John. I can't just leave without telling Lia. I need to write a note. Let her know what happened. Say good-bye."

He nodded.

Quickly Amry pulled a piece of paper from her notebook and sat to write the hardest letter she'd ever written.

My Dearest Lia,

I am so sorry that fate has separated us for our last words after all these years. Please know that you are the reason I made it through all this time. You would always say that I saved you, but in fact, it was you who saved me. My beloved John has come for me today, every hope and dream I had has been restored.

My only wish was that I could have seen you one last time to tell you how much I truly love you. When the light comes for you and Haven, know I will be thinking of you and rejoicing knowing that you have finally reunited with your family. You are and forever shall be, my sister. Please explain to Sam and Bethany. Tell them I love them, and I was ready. Also, tell them Alex was right. If your soul is shared by one other, you will have an eternity of love.

Best friends always, with all my heart, Amry

Carefully placing the note on top of the stack of books, Amry took one last look at the library, before stepping into the light, hand in hand with John.

THE LETTER SLIPPED through Ophelia's fingers and floated to the floor. She melted down on the chair and lay her head on the table. She couldn't believe Amry was gone. A pool of water moistened her temple, and she abruptly raised her head. Smearing the liquid on the table, she brushed it across her fingertips. Her eyelashes felt heavy, and she took the back of her hands and rubbed them across her lids—tears. She had been crying real tears. Thoughts racing, she pushed the chair back with such force, it toppled back and on its side. All she could think about was Haven.

In a blink she was at the theater. Haven was sitting in between Bethany and Sam, laughing profusely. The credits were rolling, and the lights came up.

"Ophelia. You missed it, it was so funny." The little girl flashed a toothy grin.

"I know. I have seen it. They are a bunch of goofs, aren't they?"

"Yes."

"Listen, I need to talk with Sam and Bethany. Could you please wait in the lobby for me? But do not go anywhere."

"All right, Ophelia."

She waited until Haven left before telling her friends the news.

"Amry's gone. The light came for her when she was in the library, and it brought John with it."

"Who's John?" The two asked

"The love of her life. The boy she thought she had lost for good. She left a letter explaining she was sorry she couldn't see us before leaving, but it was time, and she was finally ready."

"Oh. I'll miss her so much," Bethany sighed.

"There's something else."

"Tell us, Ophelia."

"I think my time and Haven's time is coming. Strange things happened in the library. I had tears, real ones. And I could feel my heartbeat. But not like before. This was real. I heard it."

"I'm ... happy, and yet so sad. I'm sorry, that's wrong to say," Sam professed.

"No, I understand. I felt the same way when I read Amry's letter. I need to keep Haven close. In fact, I should go. Will you guys stay with us?"

"Of course. We don't want to lose two friends without saying goodbye."

"I'd like to take her back to my dorm room. That's where Amry and I would dream of what would come next. I'll feel close to her, and you guys. How many times did we have nights of endless laughter in that room?"

"Too many to try and count. I'm so happy we got to know you, and Amry. And Haven. She's so adorable, Ophelia. I'm overcome with joy that you two found each other again," said Sam.

"Come on, let's go." Ophelia floated towards the door.

They picked Haven up from the lobby and the four of them slowly glided across campus. It wasn't long before the light found its way to the sisters.

In the center of the room, the ball grew until it was big enough for the girls to step through. A fine mist clouded the view, but Ophelia could sense others waiting for them. Haven however, hid behind her sister, her little body trembling.

"Oh, baby girl, do not be afraid. Do you know who is waiting for us?"

"Who?" Haven's voice cracked.

"Mother and Father. They've been waiting a long time to see us. I know you want to see them, too. You hold my hand. I promise I won't let anything happen to you. All right?"

Haven slowly nodded.

Ophelia turned to Sam and Bethany; whose expressions bore the full scope of their sadness.

"I love you guys so much. I will miss you more than you could ever imagine."

"We love you, too. Maybe one day, we'll all find each other again," Bethany whispered.

"I hope so." Ophelia hugged them. "Can you do something for me? Will you let Alex know what happened? Tell him we finally found home."

"We will. And Lia, we made our decision too. The next time the light comes for us, we're going together." Sam half-smiled.

Ophelia wiped the tears from her eyes. Her friends would be happy, too. That's all she ever wanted for them. That's all Amry ever wanted for any of them. Picking up her little sister, Ophelia clutched Haven close to her chest. Mouthing one last, *I love you,* to her friends, she and Haven disappeared in the mist.

ALEX STEPPED out of the shower and wrapped himself in a fuzzy towel. The steam on the mirror lay like a thick blanket, and he wiped it away with his hand in a circular motion. Standing in the glass looking back at him was Sam and Zachary.

Startled, Alex jumped back.

"Not that it's not great to see you guys, but a little privacy would be nice."

"Oh yeah, sorry man." Sam turned his back toward the mirror.

Zachary followed his lead.

While Alex quickly dried off and slipped on some boxers, sweats, and a T-shirt, they explained how Amry reunited with John, and Ophelia's message to him before she and Haven made their journey home. Alex pushed back the tears trying to escape, before turning around to the guys.

"All done. How are you and Ruby doing?"

Zachary pivoted around. "Her benevolence has won over my uncle and just about everyone she meets. I did not realize how much it affected me when I thought she died. The idea that anyone would sacrifice themselves for me...I was consumed with guilt that had been festering and growing into the ugliness that could have eventually blackened my soul. Exactly what the demons wanted. But her robust approach to everything she does is contagious. She is slowly chipping away at my guilt and replacing it with hope."

Alex high fived the air.

"You really are a dork, McKenna," Zachary laughed.

"Dork? Where'd you hear that?" Alex grinned.

"Oh. I taught it to him," Sam said proudly.

"And Spot? Are the students warming to him?"

"Warming to him? They practically fight over who will take care of him when Ruby is busy on campus."

"Alex. There's something Bethany wanted me to tell you," said Sam. "We've decided to take the light when it comes for us. We're hoping we luck out and you're right about love goes on and being together."

"I think Amry and John are proof of that."

"Yeah man, we were thinking the same thing."

"I'm so happy for you both." Alex ran his fingers through his hair.

"Zachary, what about the demons? I mean they gotta still be lurking. Does your uncle think he can do anything about it?"

"He thinks as he has always thought, the lighter, the less darkness, the safer I remain. My powers are growing but they draw from good and that will deem me unattractive for the dwellers of the shadows."

"Never forget that."

"I shall not."

Sam stepped closer to the rim of the connection, "And you and Margaret? Any new cases since returning home?"

"Thankfully, things have been pretty quiet. Except for annoying little boys who interrupt when I'm talking." Alex glanced to his left. Jacob, the ghost of a little six-year-old boy who had taken up permanent residence in the La Boccetta house, was tugging at his shirt. "Jacob, this is Sam and Zachary. Guys, this is the precocious, Jacob O'Reilly."

"Alex. Alex." The boy continued to pull on Alex's T-shirt, stretching it out at the bottom.

"Hey, you're stretching out my shirt. Give me a few minutes and I'll call for you."

"I can't wait."

Zachary and Sam covered their mouths trying to contain their laughter. Alex rolled his eyes. "Thanks guys … you're so helpful."

"Okay kiddo, what's the burning urgency?"

"Are they from the school? The Academy of Souls?" Jacob scooted closer to the vanity and hopped up onto the counter. Sliding closer to the mirror, almost kissing it with his nose. "You guys are, aren't you?"

"Yup, we go to the Academy, little man." Sam grinned.

"Can I go?"

Alex jerked his head toward the boy. "I thought you wanted to go to your parents."

"I do. But I'm scared to go to the light. You know that—silly Alex. Their school sounds fun."

"Alex huffed a long breath. "Help me out here guys."

Zachary spoke softly, "I know it may seem to you like a place you would want to be, and there are many good souls here. However, they are all trying to go home to the light. Jacob, you have nothing to fear about the end of your journey. It sounds to me like you have family waiting, the longer you delay going to them, the sadder they will be. The Academy of Souls is just a place like any other, where we wait to complete our cycle. Why prolong your reunion with your parents just to make another temporary stop?"

The little boy retracted from the mirror and slid down to the floor. Head down, he murmured, "I guess."

Alex crouched down to eye level with him, "Listen little

guy, you can't leave. I need you. Well, until your light comes again."

"You do?" His eyes grew wide.

"Of course, I do. Look how many times you helped? What about Kyle from school?"

"That's right!" Jacob twirled.

"You showed that bully a thing or two, scared the hell out of him."

Jacob giggled. "Okay Alex, I'll stay and help you until it's time."

"Great. Now let me finish up here and then we can talk about your recent pranks on my little brother." Jacob lowered his, "Oh you heard."

"I did. And you know ..."

Before Alex could finish his sentence, the boy disappeared.

"What was that all about with your little brother?" Sam raised a brow.

"Wilby, my kid brother. He hasn't gotten his *know* yet and Jacob loves to take his things and hide them. Typical 6-year-old jokester, only this one is invisible to my brother, and it drives him crazy. Hey, any repercussion from sending Roger to *The Nowhere*?

Sam swiped his chin like he was stroking a beard, "Nope. That spaz got everything he deserved. He was delusional with a spoonful of looney. How about your great grandmother, she ever tell you how they knew each other?"

"That's funny actually. Turns out, my great-grandfather was the one to give him his travel miles to the afterlife. Vincenzo was in love with my gram and tried to kidnap her. Gramps shot him and he was as miserable in spirit as he was when he was alive. Gram didn't know he was doing such diabolical acts though. If she had, well, being shot would have been the least of his torture." Alex chuckled.

The guys were motivated by awkward silence to wrap up

the visit. "Thank you again, Alex for all your help. Everyone at the Academy cannot stop speaking about the breather that defeated the Soul Gatherer." Zachary bent at the waist.

"Oh, for the love of the gods, Zachary stop bowing. You were just as responsible as I was. In fact, you all were. We did it together, without any one of us, it wouldn't have worked."

The teens nodded, "Good-bye, Alex."

Alex stood gazing at his reflection. Life was good. He was good. His journey was just getting started. His excitement percolated again when he remembered Margaret was waiting for him in his bedroom. He couldn't wait to tell her the news.

"Hey *Tesoro*, you're not going to believe what just happened," he shouted.

"I don't know, but if involves leaving this room—forget it." *Yup. He really loves that girl.*

ACKNOWLEDGMENTS

For Cooper ... the most consistent and loyal soul that has given me love, strength, and laughter. You are my forever boy.

I'd like to thank my daughter, Stevie Aubuchon-Mendoza, for weathering through the first line of edits with each book and not openly rolling her eyes. I know you want to.

ABOUT THE AUTHOR

Originally from New York, Vicki-Ann is an award-winning author and short screenplay writer. She currently resides in Nevada. Writing Young Adult paranormal, she finds inspiration from events that have been in her life for as long as she can remember. Inheriting the sensitivity to the supernatural from her family, they continue to be an endless source of vision.